Ne

"Explores the hang-ups associated with
starting Secondary school ... laced with
humorous asides and a fast-moving plot, it
hits the right spot for this age group."
Books for your Children

Theresa Breslin

New School Blues

Kelpies

Kelpies is an imprint of Floris Books

First published in 1992 by Canongate Kelpies
Published in 2002 by Floris Books
Copyright © Theresa Breslin

The publisher acknowledges a Lottery grant
from the Scottish Arts Council towards the
publication of this series.

British Library CIP Data available

ISBN 0–86315–409-3

Printed in Europe

1

You know the way you look at someone and right away you decide that you like them?

It happens sometimes with relatives you've never met before — uncles especially. They come to visit, at Christmas time, or you meet at weddings or funerals, and there are those yukky ones with hair growing out of their nostrils who ask you how you're doing at school and tell you what a rough time they had. And then there are those uncles (like my Uncle Harry) who say, "And how is Mary?" and take the opportunity when shaking your hand to slip you a fiver, no questions asked. Then they wink and go on agreeing with whatever story your mother is telling them about you at that particular time, about how you went to school one day without your knickers on, or whatever. Well, it was the same the first time I saw Jamie. I just *knew* right away that we were going to hit it off.

We were all sitting in the high school assembly hall. First day, new entrants' assembly, first year at secondary school, everybody totally terrified out of their wits. Except me, of course — well, with two parents as teachers what do you expect? I had heard all this before. "This is not Grange Hill and don't let anybody here present think that it is for one minute." This person on the stage in front of us (who was wearing a black gown, for heaven's sake) had managed to work himself into a state of indignation and outrage over absolutely *nothing*. I mean he was putting ideas into people's heads. Some of these kids I had been all through primary school with. Their conception of breaking school rules was to throw a sweet paper down

in the playground. They were stunned. I mean
absolutely. Here he was, I assumed he was the head
teacher (nobody had actually said, I suppose it was a
bit like God, you were just supposed to know), raving
on about smoking in the toilets, or rather *not* smoking
in the toilets, going into town at lunchtime, consorting
(*consorting*?) with members of the opposite sex etc.,
etc. These children did not know what he was talking
about. They did not know what the opposite sex con-
sisted of, though half of them were it.

I exclude here for the record Margritte McGoldrick
who, as we all know, told Mrs Cult, our drama teacher,
when we were in primary three infant school, that she
was pregnant. As she had been chosen to play the
Virgin Mary in the school's nativity play, this caused
quite a stir, as you may imagine. She was of course
compelled to stand down. I was understudy for the part
and managed to step in at the last minute, with,
although I say so myself, a very moving and sympathetic performance. Mrs Cult gave me a very strange
look at the party after the show. Goodness knows what
Margritte had been telling her. After all it was *she* who
asked *me* about the facts of life. Was it my fault if she
misunderstood?

Well, anyway, as I was saying, Batman was going on
and on, and swishing backwards and forwards on the
stage with his cloak for dramatic effect. Everyone was
sitting bolt upright on their seats in the assembly hall
with their arms folded, myself included, when I noticed
off to the left-hand side someone who was definitely
not paying attention.

I took my glasses off and pretended to polish them
carefully, so that I could adjust my seat and line of
vision to see what he was up to. Not one of ours, I
thought. Castle Secondary School had three or four

feeder primaries and this first year pupil could not possibly be from St Ann's. More like a Spindle Street inmate, I thought. The "wrong" side of town. I put my glasses back on, folded my arms and sat back in my seat. I had picked a chair at the back of the hall and on the aisle for a quick getaway. He was opposite at the end of his row, and was amusing himself by untying the tyres of the girls' regulation school dresses in front of him and retying them to the spars of the chairs they were sitting on. He had done that about four or five times before he sensed someone was watching him and looked across. Our gazes met, instant rapport. I gave him my Japanese camp commandant look with my rimless glasses. He dropped his eyes.

The assembly went on ... We were being allocated our classes. I could hardly wait to see if we would be put together. He had taken out a penknife and was fiddling about with the blades. Names were called with class numbers and we were given form teachers. We shuffled out to the various form rooms following our particular teacher. It took a little longer for those girls who were inexplicably attached to their chairs. When we arrived at a particularly drab classroom with peeling posters of "Drugs are for Mugs" and "Cycle Safety" on the walls, I looked around quickly. He was already lounging in a chair at the back, the penknife still in his hand. Right on!

"I am your form teacher, Mr Wilkins. I am glad to see that most of you at any rate are in school uniform."

I gave Mr Wilkins an encouraging smile and blinked at him intelligently from behind my glasses.

"... though some of you are not ..."

I glanced across at Jamie. He was definitely in the "are not ..." category. Scuffed trainers, trousers with a tear in them, shirt hanging out and a very worn

jumper. By contrast I had on my newly purchased gingham dress, blue cardi and navy shoes carefully polished by mummy.

Mr Wilkins beamed at me. "Now I want you all to
get to know each other as soon as possible. It is a bit
strange for all you primary children being thrown
together in the big school. Just choose anyone, anyone
at all, or someone you think that you would get along
with and go and introduce yourself."

"My opportunity," I thought. We were obviously
twin souls. I could not mistake that look he had given
me in the assembly hall. Together we were going to
liven up first year and Mr Wilkins. I went across
immediately.

"Hello," I said, enunciating all my vowels and conso-
nants perfectly, "I am Mary McPherson." I extended
my hand in greeting as all well-brought-up children
should. "How do you do?"

He looked up from where he was cleaning his finger-
nails with the blade of his penknife. "Bog off," he said.

2

"Earrings," Mr Wilkins was bearing down on us on the starboard side, "are not allowed in this school. That is, they are, but only for girls. I'll overlook it today," he addressed Jamie, "but please don't wear them tomorrow. Boys don't wear earrings," he added encouragingly.

I could have pointed out here that:
(a) that was a sexist remark and
(b) it was also factually inaccurate
but I was interested in observing how my new friend was going to handle this. He did not let me down.

"Have to, sir," he sniffed, fingering the gold stud, silver hoop and green enamel miniature skull which decorated his left ear lobe. "It's my acupuncture treatment, stimulates my nerve endings. I got to keep them in all the time."

"Have to, son, have to," Mr Wilkins corrected his grammar. "Why?"

"Why 'have to,' sir?" said Jamie blankly.

"Why are you having acupuncture treatment?" Mr Wilkins asked patiently.

"To help me give up smoking, sir. It's the only thing that's worked so far."

Jamie gave Mr Wilkins the look that Lizzie Borden gave the judge.

Mr Wilkins had been a form teacher for a long time. "Fine, son," he said. "Bring in a note from your parents and family doctor to that effect. Otherwise they will be confiscated." He walked to the front of the classroom and pulled open a drawer in his desk. "While we are on the subject you all might as well see what I call 'the Chamber of Horrors.'"

He laughed at his own joke (most teachers do). "In here are all the items which I have confiscated over the years. It will serve as a guide to you new entrants to what will not be tolerated."

He boomed this last phrase out and thumped his desk. Several pupils twitched nervously.

"Offensive wearing apparel," he held up a tee-shirt with a slogan imprinted on it which I could not possibly repeat. "Disgusting playthings," he displayed a slime ball and two green zit sweets. "And dangerous weapons."

Jamie sat up in his seat and began to take notice.

"A flick comb, electric body stunner, catapult ..." Mr Wilkins intoned ...

"Good grief!" I thought. Obviously most of the pupils at this school had progressed straight to the Secure Unit at Barlinnie Prison.

"So, you all understand." Mr Wilkins gazed round the classroom. "You are here to work."

I nodded vigorously. I had been told this often enough by my parents. I glanced across at Jamie. He was playing with his penknife again. And what he had not seen was that Mr Wilkins had also noticed him playing with his penknife.

"For instance," said Mr Wilkins slowly and in sorrow. "there comes a time when 'first day or not first day' we have to make an example."

The acupuncture scam had really got to him. Jamie whittled away head down, not realizing the doom which was about to fall.

Mr Wilkins descended. "Now this," he said, retrieving the knife from Jamie's hand, "is what I would call a suspect object."

I acted immediately. As I explained to Jamie later, it was our only hope.

"My Guide knife," I shrieked snatching it from his hand. 'thank you *so* much. I thought I had lost it. Captain would have been so disappointed with me. I only got it last week, and it is so useful. You can do all sorts with it. Look, see, it has little scissors, and a thing for taking stones out of horses' hooves." I babbled on. Did he believe me? He did.

"Guides," he said. "Excellent, excellent. My wife, Mrs Wilkins" (what else would his wife be called?) "is Akela of the local cub pack."

He looked at Jamie. He was wasting his time. That was not Boy Scout material. Anyone could see that a mile off.

He walked back to the front of the class.

I winked at Jamie. He ignored me.

Mr Wilkins busied himself in the time that was left in giving out timetables, dinner rotas, school plans and general behaviour guides. The bell rang. What next? I consulted my timetable. History, wherever that was. We filed out of the classroom.

I would have to choose my opportunity to return the penknife. I worked my way closer to Jamie in the corridor. I felt sorry for him. Such an amateur! They would quickly find out who had done the mischief in the assembly hall this morning. He had already lost two Brownie points with the earrings and smoking scam, and soon he would have to face up to tying girls to chairs. One thing I had learnt, early on, was to make sure that at least three other people should look responsible when something went wrong. Witness Denise Flynn, the most gullible child I know, she just happened to be standing there when the shining star of Bethlehem crashed on top of the Three Wise Men. I had earlier given her a few tips on how to work the wire contraption which the janitor had rigged up to

move the star across the stage. Denise is one of my
very best friends. Would I tell her anything which
might get her into trouble? I never actually touched it.
I wasn't even there when it landed on the Magi knock-
ing Banharjee McPartlin right off his papier mâché
camel.

I had manoeuvred myself beside Jamie by the time
we reached the history class and it was fairly easy to
slip into the seat beside him.

I nudged him. "Interested in acquiring a knife?" I
enquired.

Then I looked at him with new respect. In bumping
up against him I became aware that he was carrying
something. Before leaving the form room, he had managed (and later both of us were to be grateful for it) to
acquire something. Out of Wilkie's "Chamber of
Horrors" Jamie had palmed the electric body stunner.

3

"Give us it," said Jamie holding out his hand.

Never argue with someone who has a stun gun, that's my motto. I handed him his knife at once. "Just remember who conned Wilkie out of it, thanks very much."

"Right. Okay. Thanks, metalmouth," he said grudgingly.

I clamped my lips together immediately. I had forgotten about the blasted braces. Usually I am much more careful, taking pains not to smile and speaking with my mouth open barely two centimetres. That way and if I move my head about a lot people hardly notice. My father says it's like trying to have a conversation with a Swahili-speaking giraffe. But then that shows that my father has as much sensitivity as a Sherman tank — a thing my mother keeps telling him. Well, he did buy her an oven glove and a dish-towel for their first wedding anniversary. He would never do that again now that she's started her Female Assertiveness classes.

"Are you all here? Good," said the figure at the front of the class.

The teacher? He was much more interesting than Mr Wilkins or any of the white-blouse, navy-skirt brigade from primary school. This one was well past his "sell-by" date.

He had on a lilac sweatshirt with a hole in the elbow, reddish checked trousers and odd socks. I looked again — yes, definitely, odd socks. Had anyone else noticed? I glanced around. A significant number of the class was absent. Doggers? On the first day? Picked off by snipers in the corridor? What was worrying me was that it was mainly the St Ann intake which was AWOL. No street sense at all. They couldn't negotiate a set of stairs, two corridors and one corner. The Spindle Streeters seemed all present and correct.

"I am Mr Dow." He stopped and rummaged about on the top of his desk and found a pair of glasses and put them on. He then picked up the register and scrutinized it carefully. "Where are the rest of you?" he asked. "Of course, you wouldn't really know, would you?" He threw the register and his glasses back on to the desk. "Mmmmmm." He went to the door. "Better leave this open for stragglers." He looked up and down the corridor. "Right, no doubt every class you go into today you will receive a lecture on what to do and what not to do. Well I'm not going to give you a lecture. However, you are here to work ..."

I switched off.

They all trailed in eventually like Bruce's camp followers coming over the hill.

"I got lost, sir."

"I couldn't find the escalator to this floor."

The *escalator*. Where did they think they were? Harrods?

"A big boy told me to go through the doors at the end of the corridor and take the first left after the swimming pool."

I closed my eyes and groaned. Good grief! They hadn't actually fallen for the swimming pool/escalator rubbish. Any infant knows in first year at secondary you never, ever ask an older pupil for directions. And if you are really desperate the only person in the whole school who knows what's happening is the janitor.

"I went to the toilet and when I came out everyone had gone and left me," sobbed Deirdre Glissop.

Jamie sniggered. This was so embarrassing. They were all St Ann pupils. Thick as mince. I mean, if you did something like that the last thing you would do is *admit* to it.

Mr Dow ran his fingers through his hair. "Eh, well, sit down now." He pulled a manky hanky from his pocket and gave it to Deirdre Glissop. He could hardly keep his face straight. "Weren't you all given maps and instructions by your form teacher? And didn't you all come up for visits last term when you were in primary seven?"

"And hasn't it not made the slightest bit of difference?" I added under my breath.

"Your map is upside down, dear." He addressed the child who had been vainly searching for a swimming pool in a pre-war state comprehensive. "Look, where it says here, 'top,' that means that bit is at the top."

He glanced at his watch. "Right, it is nearly lunchtime. I am going to let you out early, but you *must not* tell anyone. I just don't want you caught in the rush when the bell goes. The dinner hall is at the far end of the bottom corridor." He looked at the class. 'tell you what. I'll take you there myself. Come on."

We almost made it. We must have been only fifty yards short of the swing doors leading into the dinner hall when the lunchtime bell rang.

Nothing had prepared me for it. Not both parents giving me masses of handy hints, not my careful questioning of the twins next door who were in third year, not my reconnoitring of the premises during the school holidays so that I would not be caught wrong-footed, and certainly not the three meticulously planned primary/secondary liaison induction days. Imagine standing under Niagara Falls, or trying to get on a lifeboat from the *Titanic*, or riding the wrong way during the

Charge of the Light Brigade. Classroom doors crashed open and bodies poured out from every direction. Bags were used as battering rams as the starving charged towards food. The Bolshevik Bread Riots must have resembled this. I was going under when I felt a hand grab the neck of my dress and I was pulled firmly up against the wall safely inside the dinner hall only three short of the top of the queue at the serving hatch.

I looked round to thank my rescuer.

"Okay, metalmouth?" asked Jamie.

"Okay," I said.

4

"Look upon it as an initiative test," said Mr Brown our English teacher as he distributed jotters, exercise books, notebooks and folders. "Finding your way about the school for the first few days will give you a chance to practise for the Standard Grade English exams which your year will eventually sit. Following instructions and asking directions will make you more articulate and increase your life skills."

I surveyed the mounting pile of stationery on my desk with alarm. Apart from the fact that my schoolbag was going to be seriously overcrowded, the volume of blank paper being handed out (which we no doubt would have to fill) indicated to me a lot of work ahead — and this for just one subject.

"All right, dear?" Mr Brown asked Deirdre briskly as he passed her desk, without waiting for an answer.

She had just arrived in the classroom, twenty minutes late for the first block in the afternoon, heavily escorted by two senior prefects. She had come out of the toilets after lunchtime and (again) found that the "whole school had disappeared." Her recourse this time, as she had lost her map and had no idea where she was supposed to be, was to sit on the stair and sob quietly, until discovered by the Bozos who were no doubt policing the area for the smokers mentioned in this morning's assembly. Apart from her obvious bladder problem Deirdre seemed to have what Mr Brown termed "no spatial awareness." We took that to mean that she did not know where she was. She certainly appeared rather confused as she sat there red-eyed doing nothing while everyone else carefully wrote their name, address, class number, school name, school address and anything else they could think of on all these books we were being given.

"Pick up your pen, dear, and write your name on your books," he said to her firmly. "You do remember your name? If not, it will be on your bus pass, you can copy it from there."

Well! He was a bit crisp. No sympathy there. I mentally crossed him off the list of possibilities for forged notes from parents for leave of absence, "forgetting" homework etc., etc. I could see Jamie had done the same. He had picked up his pen and was writing in this jotter. He passed it to me. It read, "this guy is a mean machine and will have to be dealt with."

I nodded and passed it back. Privately I thought any dealing could be done by Jamie. I intended to steer well clear of Mr Brown. As it turned out, I pitched right in there when Jamie eventually did "deal with him."

In front of me Deirdre was sniffing into her hanky. She was being careful to be loud enough to be noticed and enlist the sympathy of the class, but not loud enough to cause a disturbance — operating at what you might call "teacher tolerance level."

Mr Brown had really intimidated her. I, for one, was extremely grateful. With the slightest encouragement she could get right out of hand. Well I remember the bawling she started up when as Lead Shepherd she was made responsible for the donkey in the stable.

To let you understand, I was *not* in the huff because Mrs Cult, our drama instructor, wouldn't let me ride the donkey across the stage, even although she should have let me. After all, the donkey was a matter of historical record (and she was the one who wanted authenticity). I pointed it out to her in a Bible story. It specifically says that Mary *rode* on the donkey to Bethlehem.

Now, I don't really want to go into it here, exactly what it was the donkey did in the stable. It is enough for you to know that later, a substantial amount of senna pods were found mixed in with the bran in its feedbag. Deirdre completely lost the head. She should never have been put in charge of the donkey in the first place, and anyway, Mrs Cult had been warned many times about the hazards of having live animals on stage. But she wanted authenticity, she said. "A living Christmas pageant, real action." Those were her very words.

Well, she certainly got it. It had required all my acting skills to keep the proper look of spiritual ecstasy on my face, as Mary, having just given birth to the Son of God. It was really me who kept the show going at that point, due to my presence of mind, and not because, as Mrs Cult hinted darkly afterwards, *some* people could keep right on acting, as it might not have come as a surprise to *them* what was going to happen.

"These *must* be covered," Mr Brown said, "with strong paper. These are your textbooks. You have to look after them. *No* replacements will be issued if they are lost."

He paused at Deirdre's desk and gave her a look which suggested that he thought she would be the type of child who would lose a book. She stopped sniffing immediately and shoved her hanky in her pocket.

"These are your home readers, although I expect you are all members of your local library." He looked at some of the Spindle Street Specials and sighed. "If not, go and join at once. Why should I be the only person to have to put up with you?" he muttered under his breath.

I took an interest in the reading books. This would let me know just how "comprehensive" this school was. I was convinced there would be secret grading methods. Spies and secret messages from the primary school, marks beside our names. For "Annabel has a vivid imagination and is capable of creative thought" read "this child is a right little liar." Goodness knows what St Ann's headmistress had to say about me. I checked around me. Let's see who would be getting *War and Peace* and who was stuck with *Topsy and Tim Visit the Dentist*.

They were all the same. *Simon's Challenge* by Theresa Breslin. I flicked through a few pages. It looked good.

5

I could barely keep up with Jamie as we came out of the school gate together at home-time. I must have had about three tons of textbooks in my bag. And it didn't help that it was still a stupid schoolbag from primary. My mother had insisted that it was perfectly serviceable and had refused to buy me a new one. I looked enviously at Jamie's rucksack. That was the perfect answer. Everything stuffed in, weight equally distributed and hands free for use in the scrum. He was walking quickly down the road away from the school which was in the older part of the town.

"Where do you stay?" I asked him.

"Up the Gravey."

"Where's that exactly?"

"Next to the graveyard. My mum works there part-time."

"In the *graveyard*?" (Talk about meeting interesting people!)

"Yeh. Why not?"

"Why not?" I agreed.

"She doesn't actually *bury* people. She tends the graves, a kind of gardener."

I made a mental note of this. Mr Brown said we might have to interview people at some point. I had thought of my Uncle Harry, certainly not "your parents or grandparents" as he had suggested. But there sounded as though there might be a lot of scope in Jamie's mother.

"Part-time?" I enquired.

"Yeh. She's on shifts in the bottling factory."

I made a mental note to omit this info when being

grilled later by my parents. They always have to have full biographical details of any friends I made. Although most of the Scottish economy was based on whisky it seemed to be more socially acceptable to drink the stuff than actually be involved in packaging it.

"What's your dad do?" I asked.

"Haven't a clue," said Jamie and disappeared through a hole in the hedge.

"Where are you going?" I stuck my head through after him. "You can't just go charging through people's gardens and hedges."

"I'm not. If you were as observant as you pretend to be, you would see that this opening is where one hedge stops and another starts. Look, see, there are two different hedges. One is privet and the other is beech. They have just grown close together over the years."

I squeezed through. Immediately below me was a ditch then a lane over rough ground, which led down to a field at the end. "Where does it go?"

"It's a shortcut to the graveyard. Are you coming?"

If it took us out to the graveyard then I certainly was. It would cut a half mile off my walk home. I was in the new houses at the other end of town, far out, but nor far enough out to qualify for a bus pass. My kindly parents had told me they would drop me off at the town in the morning on their way to their school, but as I finished at half-three and they didn't stop until four, I could walk home.

I followed Jamie down the lane. There was masses of heather out, purply blue, and long foxgloves taller than both of us.

"It's like the 'Secret Garden,'" I said.

"Well, it shouldn't be. My mum says that the council

are supposed to maintain it. She says she is going to complain."

"Oh, no! That would ruin it. It's better the way it is."

"Yeh, that's what I think. This way it's *my* path and only a few other people know about it. Anyway she keeps saying she'll do it but she never does. She does that with lots of things."

We had reached the gate leading into the field. Jamie climbed quickly over it.

"Is this okay?" I asked.

"Yeh, yeh. It's a new farmer that bought the land a few months ago who put this up. It was never here before he came. He's also put a whole pile of rubbish up against the old stile on the other side of the field where it goes over the back wall of the graveyard. Come on."

Jamie was halfway across the field by the time I had negotiated the gate. What with a gingham dress and a stupid satchel, I was lagging behind and completely failed to notice the movement at the left-hand bottom corner of the field.

I picked up my schoolbag and swung it a few times round my head to get momentum and then hurled it as far in front of me as possible. It would save me carrying it a few yards and it also might be so badly damaged that a replacement would be necessary. I could always say it had been a casualty in the dinner hall assault course.

"Hey, Jamie! Watch out," I shouted, and waved my hands above my head. On thinking about this later I realized that it was at this point in time I had taken one step closer to eternity. My actions almost placed me permanently on the other side of the graveyard wall, giving Jamie's mother one more little plot to tend.

The bag crashed to the ground beside Jamie and burst open. Books, jotters, pens and pencils spewed out across the grass.

"I don't think Mr Brown had this in mind when he told us to take good care of our books," said Jamie turning round and jumping out of the way.

We were both laughing so loudly that we didn't hear the sound that could have given us the couple of extra seconds which we were going to need so desperately.

I bent down to collect my books, and in doing so allowed Jamie to see past me down the length of the field.

A strangled sound came out of his throat.

I turned round.

Charging down the field towards us, throwing up great clods of earth, head down, horns extended, was an enraged five-ton bull.

6

"*Run!*" screamed Jamie.

It's amazing how human beings react when faced with a situation of unparalleled terror. Bravery, quiet calm, quick-wittedness — I displayed none of these. My legs gave way and I sank to my knees clutching the last thing I was replacing in my schoolbag. It happened to be the apron and dish-towel which my mother had insisted I take to school in case we got home economics on the first day. Now, you must realize I thought I was about to be creamed by several megatons of moving beef, so I was not thinking too clearly.

(Though later, when I had more time to analyze my actions, I thought perhaps this had been an instinctive gesture on my part. I can trace my family, on my mother's side, back to the time the Armada was wrecked off the Scottish coast and some of the sailors settled here. I do have Spanish blood in me and my Uncle Harry agreed that I could have been unconsciously trying a toreador's pass with the dish-towel being the matador's red cape. My father snorted when he heard this and said if I had Spanish blood, he was a Chinaman, and anyway, an Aberdeen Angus was not going to join in the spirit of the Corrida the same way as a Spanish fighting bull — I told you my father had no sensitivity.)

I closed my eyes and prepared to die.

"*Christmas crackers!*" shouted Jamie.

There was a micro-second's pause, a crack and a grunting sound, and then I felt the now familiar sensation of my neck being grabbed and I was being dragged across the field.

"*Move!* Will you? Jamie yelled in my ear.

My legs were working again and I moved.

We reached the graveyard wall and legged it over.

"What happened?" I asked. We were sitting on a grave on the other side. "Kathleen Campbell, aged six, died of measles, 1874. Sadly missed." I didn't think she would mind.

Jamie levered himself up on Kathleen's tombstone and peered over the wall. I joined him. The bull was in the middle of the field, pawing and stamping and shaking its head from side to side.

"I zapped it with my stun gun," said Jamie.

"You did?"

I readjusted my glasses and gazed at him with new respect.

"Yeh, it was enough to hold it until we got clear but I dropped the gun. Look."

The bull was grinding up the body stunner, tramping it into the earth with its hooves.

"It will never be any good now." Jamie jumped back down from the wall. "Best thing I ever had," he said sadly.

"Sorry," I said.

I picked up my bag. For some reason I had held onto this repulsive object in my flight. They say in times of trial you cling to things you love. That shows you what a lie that is.

We limped through the graveyard.

"Wait till I tell my mother," stormed Jamie. 'she will be furious. He has no right to put his bull in that field. We could have been killed."

"It is his field, isn't it?" I asked. Personally I had no intention of telling my parents anything about this. I found that they invariably took any side except mine. I was going to be busy explaining the mangled schoolbag and the general state of my person without complicating matters with stories of wild bulls and trespassing on other people's property.

"There is no law of trespass in Scotland," said Jamie's mother. "And anyway, it wouldn't apply in this case, because that is a right of way."

We were sitting round the table in the kitchen of their cottage, a little stone building outside the west wall of the graveyard.

"I am not walking two miles to school every morning," said Jamie. "So he can get his blasted animal out of that field pronto."

"Don't exaggerate," said his mother. "It is only about a mile and a half to the school and you can always take your bike."

I liked Jamie's mum, and their cottage. It was very old with a range and a flagstone floor. Jamie said his great-grandfather had built it. He had been a gravedigger and actually caught real bodysnatchers. There were letters and papers to prove it, he said, when I laughed.

Jamie's mother was a woman of many parts. Not only did she bottle whisky and tend graves, she also sculpted. However, not for her the artist's smock and the paint-smudged nose. She had on dungarees with a hole in them and bits of wire hanging out the pocket. In a corner of the kitchen was the sculpture she was working on. She told me she was trying to get away from the traditional style funeral monument, stone cherubs and skulls and things like that. She wanted to re-educate the burying public into a new awareness of steel and plastic as a valid statement on modern death, with perhaps an underlying trace of humour. She was also hoping that someone would pay her a great deal of money for it. It was hard to say what her sculpture resembled. The main part looked a bit like the old metal and rubber refuse containers that our black bin-bags used to go in.

I didn't actually tell her that of course, so I just said I thought it was very nice. And she patted my shoulder and asked if anyone close to me had died recently. All I could think of at the time was that if Jamie hadn't nicked the stun gun from Wilkie, that could have been his everlasting monument.

"I'd better go," I said. "Thanks for the biscuits and juice."

"I'll go up and see the new farmer tonight," said Jamie's mum. "I should really have spoken to him ear-lier when he put up the gate and piled the rubble up at the old stile. He probably doesn't realize that people use the path across his field. It will be all quickly sorted out."

Little did we realize at the time that, far from being "quickly sorted out," we were all going to have a fight on our hands.

7

"Two hair ribbons lost, your spectacles twisted out of shape, a button missing from the back of your dress and the hem torn, shoes muddied and scraped and the schoolbag almost destroyed. Really, Mary, I thought all this would stop when you went to secondary school. When are you going to grow up and become a lady?"

My mother was ranting on at the dinner table while I tried to eat in peace. I had thought I might arrive home before them and get cleaned up, but no such luck. They rolled up just as I was getting my key in the door. I had attempted to remove the majority of the muck and grass in Jamie's house but there was not much I could do about the rest.

"Honestly, Jack, can't you speak to her?" My parents exchanged glances across the table. This was my very favourite of the many parental manoeuvres which they indulged in. Talking about me as though I was not there. It really bugged my brains. They wouldn't like it if I did it to them. The only trouble was being an only child made this difficult.

"Mary is just about to tell us all about her day. Aren't you, pet?"

My father put his knife and fork down. "Come on then, tell us how you manage to come looking as though you have done fifteen rounds with Barry McGuigan. Give us an action replay."

"More like edited highlights," I thought to myself. I hadn't noticed Jamie's mother going on and on at him over the state of his clothes. Mind you his clothes were not too neat to begin with.

"It was an interesting day," I started. (With some

bits more interesting than others.) "Do you know anything about rights of way?"

"Rights of way?" my father repeated.

The two of them looked at each other blankly.

"What's that got to do with anything?" asked my
mother. "Oh, I know — it's a project, isn't it?" (Well, it
was, sort of.) "That's a good sign, homework to do on
the first day. We can go to the library later, they should
have information of that kind there."

My father picked up his knife and fork and started
eating again.

"Lovely casserole, dear," said my mother.

My father nodded complacently.

My mother's flattery was transparent. They took
turns to make the dinner, and tonight's culinary disaster was my father's. The casserole was disgusting.
Waxy carrots lay half-submerged in a scummy gravy
studded with lumpy bits of meat.

"How was your day?" I got that diversion tactic in
quickly.

The two of them competed to see who had had the
most tiring/exhausting/frustrating time. For the next
half-hour we had the hidden curriculum, sexism in
schools, gender differentiation and staffroom politics.

"Did you make any new friends?" my mother asked
as we cleared up.

I told her about Jamie and his mother but was vague
about the rest.

Later, as I brushed my teeth, I inspected the state of
play *re* the braces. Even with my mouth closed they
bulged through my lips, causing me pain, both physical
and mental. The inside of my mouth was still raw. The
wax which the orthodontist had given me to act as a
buffer hardly worked at all. I grinned fiendishly in the
mirror. The tightening wire and their metal emplace-

ments gleamed back. They were like some medieval instruments of torture.

In my room I sorted out my books and jotters into subject piles. "Cover them carefully," Mr Brown had said. Some of mine would need major surgery.

I laid out my clothes for the morning and selected a different pair of glasses. I suppose that in terms of my vision my parents were doing their best. When it was discovered that my eyesight needed correction my mother had let me choose several different styles. This was in case I would become depressed at having to wear spectacles. Actually I didn't really mind. I looked in my dressing table mirror. You could change your personality so easily using them as a prop. I selected a thick black pair. Tomorrow I would be the Proclaimers.

"When you gooooooo will you send back a letter from Americaaaaaa ..." I sang as I jumped into bed. I had the booklet which we had borrowed from the library.

Rights of Way, published by the Rights of Way Society.

"Most Scottish rights of way have their roots deep in the past," it said. "They are the old cross-country routes, many being 'drove roads' on which cattle and sheep were driven to market; others were 'kirk' or 'coffin' roads."

I adjusted my glasses.

"The common law recognizes a public need for routes from one place to another."

Well, that was reassuring.

Then they cited cases brought against landowners dating back hundreds of years. People appeared to have got shot at quite a lot in those days. Modern actions were not encouraged it seemed. That was gloomy news. I pushed my spectacles up my nose.

After that we quickly got into the "wherefores" and

"therebys" and "subsists." My eyelids became heavy. I was almost asleep. And then I reached the section headed "Obstructions." There were several points here which Jamie would certainly be interested in I thought. I turned the page and before me in black and white were a crucial two or three sentences. I read them and re-read them. I could hardly wait until tomorrow when I could tell Jamie.

8

It wasn't until first break the next day that I got a chance to speak to Jamie. We were trying to find a space to sit down among the crowd under the stairs. Jamie elbowed his way through to the railings.

"*Ughh!* Look at that," he said.

Someone had been sick.

"That looks like exactly what they were serving in the dinner hall yesterday," someone said. "Remind me to give the Snackie a miss today."

People moved away quickly. I turned to go. Jamie caught my arm.

"It's cool," he said and picked up his piece of plastic imitation vomit, put it in his pocket and sat down. "Where's this book then?"

"Did your mum go and see the farmer?" I asked as I handed it over.

"Yeh, last night. She came back spitting blood."

I found it hard to imagine Jamie's mother spitting anything, far less blood.

"She said he just laughed. Said it was his land and he would do what he wanted, and anyway his bull was quite docile."

"Quite docile! Quite docile?" I shrieked. "It was charging us at a hundred miles an hour. If you hadn't whammed it on the nose with that thing we would both be dead."

I shuddered at the memory of what had been one of the worst experiences of my life.

"I know. I know," Jamie agreed. "I don't think my mum mentioned the electric stunner to him. She thought it wise to leave that bit out. Farmers can be

quite sensitive regarding their livestock, might have
put it off its feed or turned its milk sour."

We both laughed.

"Anyway, he said that it was probably just wandering over to have a look at us. Bulls are naturally curi-
ous and we have to stay away from his land in future. I
had to walk the long way round this morning and it
took me ages," he added bitterly.

"Wandering over to have a look at us? Wandering
over?" I was beginning to sound like a parrot. "That'll
be right. It had murderous intent that beast, a very
nasty gleam in its eye."

"I wouldn't have thought you would have noticed
the gleam in its eye," said Jamie sarcastically. "You
fainted."

"I *did not*."

I denied this hotly and looked round quickly to see if
anyone had heard him. I decided not to tell him my
theory about my instinctive bullfighter's reaction at
this point. People have a habit of not believing me
when things like that happen (apart from my Uncle
Harry, that is). Take, for instance, the bit during the
Christmas pageant when the Archangel Gabriel
brought Mary the Good News. To set the record
straight, I did *not* over-react. It was stretching credibil-
ity a bit far to imagine that, faced with such a vision, I,
as Mary, would merely bend my head in humble acqui-
escence, which was the scripted version of the play.
After all, it's not every day that an archangel, complete
with ringed halo and three-foot wings, comes flying
through your window. I mean, even in biblical times
that would be an event somewhat out of the ordinary.
My small startled gasp was quite natural. I did not, by
the way, despite what some folk may tell you, go
swooning about the stage, clutching my hand to my

brow, or *anything* like that. My Uncle Harry said it was professional jealousy from the people who suggested that I had been hamming it up.

"Have you read the part about obstructions?" I asked Jamie to take his mind off my supposed fainting. I pointed out the section I had read last night, which I thought was important.

"Yeh, it says here that a bull should not be kept on land crossed by a public right of way. But my mum went to the police station on her way back from seeing the farmer last night. She asked if the farmer was allowed to put fences up and she mentioned the bull. Don't panic," he said, seeing my horrified expression at the word "police," "she didn't give any names or details. They told her that for them to take up a case it would have to be an established right of way and they had no record of one there."

"What are we going to do now?" I asked Jamie.

"What can we do?" He shrugged his shoulders. "I'll let my mum read this book and see what she says. The trouble is with my mum," he sighed, "she means to do things but then she's always working."

I thought of my own parents who were both working. Jamie's mum would be in a slightly different position. The bottling plant wages didn't always match up to the price on the actual bottle. If Jamie's dad was AWOL then his mum would be busy finding cash for dinner money never mind the Reebok trainers.

"Mmmmm," I thought for a bit. Asking my parents would be far too complicated, and probably involve an inquisition which would end up with being banned from speaking to Jamie at all.

We tried to work our way through the book together, but it was very complicated. A member of the public could bring an action to establish a right of way, it had been done before by hillwalkers to preserve access to glens and mountains. It had been done as far back as 1849. But it appeared to be a very involved process and as the book pointed out could be expensive.

We still hadn't come up with an idea when the interval bell rang. We weren't to know that eventually we would receive help from the most unexpected source.

9

"Guidance, next block." Jamie was reading from his timetable. "If this is anything to do with Guides I'm out of here."

With my family educational background I knew of course exactly what "Guidance" entailed.

"Depending on the teacher's interpretation of guidance you might prefer the blue uniform and the woggle, old son," I thought, as our ragged band followed a triumphant Deirdre into the classroom. (Believe it or not, she had actually managed to locate the correct room at the correct time.)

Castle High School was operating a Pastoral Care Scheme. This involved each class in one block per week of Guidance, i.e. Personal and Social Development. Now this, as you can imagine, could open a whole can of worms as I knew only too well. My mother took a guidance class and in the past had involved me in preparing her lessons. Her group of pupils had, over the years, been exposed by means of role-playing to shoplifters, drug dealers, child stealers, under-age drinkers, parentless parties, etc., etc. They were probably the most streetwise bunch of kids in Britain.

Our teacher was Mrs Pollock a.k.a. the Physical Education Principal. So she had us both ways, it was a healthy mind and body and no escape.

"I am here to help you with attendance, time-keeping, behaviour and any problems you might have ..." she said brightly.

There was a collective sigh as we slumped in our seats.

"... also, things like alcohol and sex education."

Some became more alert.

"We will start with a quick glance at the school handbook."

She gave out copies of a multi-coloured booklet illustrated with cutesy line drawings of pupils doing various activities. None of them looked particularly appealing to me. Jamie nudged me. He had found the page of subject options for the end of second year. The school was part of a group offering special modules; Jamie was interested in Power Tools and Basic Soldering. I noticed one giving Saloon Practices. To do with the alcohol mentioned earlier, perhaps? Unfortunately, on reading it more carefully I realized that it was linked to the Hairdressing Module and must be a misprint.

"Something of interest, Jamie and Mary?" asked Mrs Pollock approaching us.

She knew our names already! On day two, with no introductions!

Jamie had flicked to the last page. This was a tear-off with an outline drawing of the school badge. It depicted a castle and a drawbridge.

"Ah," said Mrs Pollock, looking at it thoughtfully. She held it up to the class. "One of the beginner exercises which we can do in first year is to colour in the school badge."

There was a stunned silence (apart from Denise who gave a small squeal of delight).

"And, the page is even perforated so that when completed you can tear it out and take it home to show your parents. Or whoever," she added hurriedly, no doubt remembering the one-parent family lesson coming up later.

Jamie shook his head slowly. "No way," he mouthed silently to me.

Mrs Pollock walked back to the front of the class-room, but instead of picking up a box of coloured crayons from her table she picked up the waste-bin. She held it out in front of her as she went between the desks. All that could be heard for the next few minutes was ripping and tearing sounds. She stopped at Denise's desk and gently prised the picture from her fingers.

"Right," she said briskly, 'that's that done. Now, what next?" She hoisted herself up onto her table and put her feet on the desk in front. "I think we'll talk about me ..."

And for the next twenty minutes or so she did. Only it wasn't boring at all. She told us about her first day at school, of being terrified and feeling conspicuous with all new clothes on, and no one speaking to her, of not being able to find the toilets and getting lost.

"... and I ended up being late for a class and I was running along the corridor and the head saw me and he was wearing a big black gown and he bawled me out for running and I got to the class twenty minutes late nearly in tears ..."

"How old were you?" asked Jamie.

"Why, the same age as I am now," she said. "I have just started a new post here. Yesterday was my first day, same as you. We're in this together, pal."

10

Jamie and I trudged the long way home that night.

"I'll lend your mum that book," I offered as we came to the path to his house. To be honest I quite fancied biscuits, juice and some company again rather than a lonely wait for my parents at my house.

"Sure," he said. "She should still be home. Her shift this week doesn't start until ten."

"Ten tonight?"

"Yeh. That bottling conveyor belt never stops."

We went into the cottage. His mother was stirring something on the cooker. She looked tired.

"Did you get a sleep today?" he asked her as he slung his bag in a corner.

She sighed. "Not much, there were three funerals. I like to tidy up and sort the flowers right away. Relatives often come back later on in the day and it should look nice for them."

"Yeh," said Jamie, "the busy season's coming up."

They saw my blank look.

"Winter," explained Jamie. "Cold weather, the OAPs pop off like flies."

"Jamie!" said his mother.

She poured us some juice and we took it to Jamie's room. The cottage was very small. There were only two main rooms on the ground floor, the living-room cum kitchen and Jamie's mother's bedroom. To get to Jamie's room we had to climb up to the attic of the cottage via a slingsby ladder and through a trapdoor at the top. We stood up. I gaped.

"Doesn't your mum freak out when she sees your room like this?" I asked as we climbed over mounds of clothing, toys, model cars, planes, electronic equipment, books, jotters, paper. You name it, it was there. Jamie's mother evidently believed in children having their own space.

"Na, she never comes up here," Jamie said as he pushed a pile of stuff off a chair and sat down.

I went over and looked out the dormer window. You could see the rows of gravestones with the meticulously even paths between.

"Great view from your window," I joked.

"Isn't it?" he said enthusiastically. "It's really interesting, you can pick up all sorts of things just lying about. They are running out of space, and had to clear out a whole new area last year. I found some terrific stuff."

Jamie showed me some of the things he had found in the graveyard. I am a firm believer in personal development, each to his own, live and let live, one man's meat etc., etc. Half the trouble in the world is caused by people not minding their own business and not letting other people get on with minding theirs. Tolerance and understanding are my bywords. Who am I to comment on another person's taste?

I have never *seen* such a gross display of old relics in my life. He had bits of stone skulls and crossbones and metal crosses. There were little broken plaques with moving phrases etched on them like "Sadly Missed" and "Always Remembered." He had old maps and rubbings from tombs pinned to his wall.

I don't know whether it was the time of year or the objects we were examining, but I felt a distinct cooling of the temperature. I leaned over his bed and switched on a fan heater which was on the floor.

"Don't do that," Jamie said and switched it off at once.

"Aren't you cold?"

"A bit," he admitted, "but we can't put that on until it's really freezing."

"Why not?" I asked. (I know, I know. Definitely slow on the uptake.)

"Because our last electricity bill was three hundred and eighty pounds and they nearly cut us off," he said testily.

"Sorry."

"Yeh, we were. It took us months to pay it back. I tried to persuade my mum to get a baby."

"Eh?" I said.

"If you have a baby in the house," he explained patiently, "they are not allowed to cut off your electricity."

"You can't have a baby, just like that," I said. (Boy, did this child need his guidance classes, or what? He must have been dodging off during his health and hygiene in primary school.) "It's quite an ... er ... involved procedure ... and, it takes time."

"I am not totally stupid," said Jamie. "I know that. I meant *borrow* one, or foster someone, real quick. Anyway, she wouldn't, she's too honest."

Well, it was good to know at least one member of the family was on the side of law and order. Obviously the defective gene came from the absent father.

We went back downstairs. Jamie's mum was setting the table for dinner.

"I'd better go home," I said. "I'll phone you later and you can tell me if you think the book will help."

"Tricky, that one," laughed Jamie's mum. "We don't have a phone."

Earlier I might have thought the lack of a phone was an option they had decided on as a trendy stand against modern technology. I now realized that there were people who couldn't afford to have things I took for granted.

I could see the top of some of the monuments in the graveyard from my window. There was a slight chill in the air so I closed the window over. I suddenly thought of Jamie in *his* room. It would be quite cold in the cottage by now, and he would be on his own if his mother was doing a late shift.

I looked round my room at the colour co-ordinated curtains, wallpaper and bedspread. I had thrown fits of screaming and sulking when my room was being redecorated, my mother's taste and mine being violently opposed. I hadn't actually wanted your Adrian Mole's basic black, you understand, more of an orange and purple fresco which I had designed and was prepared to paint myself. My father said I could paint the garage roof (inside) if I had Michelangelo type urges. My mother muttered she was having an urge at that precise moment but refused to specify what exactly. I hadn't spoken to them for six whole days. Until pocket money day, if truth be told.

I could hear them in the kitchen below. I snuggled right down under my duvet.

Next day we had physical education first block. I was not looking forward to it. Contact sports are not my scene, in fact I am not really into exercise as such. I think that all this jogging and aerobics has got out of hand. My sight disability may have something to do with it. If I take my glasses off I can't see where I'm going or to whom I am passing the ball, putt, or whatever object is in use at the time. If I leave my glasses on they get all steamed up and then slide down my sweaty nose. Apart from that, my mother had refused to buy me new designer-label trainers and had insisted I pack the full school PE uniform. This school had a practice of sending groups of pupils out on road runs. Now, I'm no fashion victim but appearing in public in an airtex top and a pair of black plimsoles could seriously damage one's image. There were those of us, however, who didn't have these qualms.

"I'm desperate to get started," burbled Margritte McGoldrick. "I hope they hold trials soon. I'd love to be in the netball team."

See what I mean?

We were sitting outside the changing-room. I was dreading the next few minutes. Perhaps I could think of the perfect excuse for not having a PE kit.

I had a feeling that Mrs Pollock might be the type of teacher who would have the answers ready.

"Please Miss, my parents can't afford a PE kit" ... "Use your gear from primary school."

"I forgot it" ... "Write out 'I must not forget my PE kit' one hundred times and have it signed."

"I'm not allowed to do PE. I have this mysterious

wasting illness" ... "Where is the medical note in your folder?" etc., etc.

The fourth year charged past us towards the badminton hall. They had on tops with the school crest printed on them and black plimsoles.

We gaped. Penny blacks were in!

It was a much brighter group which confronted Mrs Pollock in the gym a few minutes later. She ranged us along the wall in a line and switched on some music. I groaned. We had had all this mood and movement stuff in primary school.

"Pretend you are a tree growing towards the sun," our primary school teacher had enthused. It had upset her quite a bit when I had rolled on the floor screaming in anguish. I thought my demonstration of a dying Rhine Forest tree blighted with acid rain was a perfectly valid interpretation. She didn't and neither did the Head.

"I am glad to see that most of you are kitted out," Mrs Pollock started. "You will find when you eventually reach your art class that you are able to print yourself a tee-shirt with the school logo on it for use in PE." She surveyed the homey airtex tops and shuddered. "A lot better than those blouses which look as though they've been found in a pre-war WRVS supply truck."

We all breathed again.

"Some knowledge of self-defence," continued Mrs Pollock, "is an almost essential requirement for today's modern woman." She paused. "The moves are, I must repeat, for *self-defence*, and would never be used to attack anyone."

Would we ever?

"Right," she waved towards the ghetto blaster. "The music will wake you up a bit this morning." She walked out onto the mat in the middle of the floor. She folded her arms. "Now, the first thing to learn is how to fall."

She demonstrated back falls and break falls. Then we moved on to dealing with an attacker, stepping back and grabbing the arm which is reaching for you. It was quite a tricky procedure to master, twisting the attacker's wrist with one hand and using your other to push the elbow down. As Mrs Pollock said, if you got it right (and we all did eventually) then bending their wrist and twisting their arm back you could produce severe pain.

It was the best PE lesson I had ever had and I do not give praise lightly.

"This should prove very useful to all of you in later life," Mrs Pollock said as she dismissed us.

Little did she know.

"I think she's wonderful," gushed Deirdre in the changing-room after, "don't you?"

Good grief! Where did she think she was? The Chalet School?

"Mmmmm?" I consulted my timetable. "She's alright, I suppose. It doesn't matter that her teeth stick out and no one would really notice the mole on the side of her cheek." (I was *not* being nasty. I personally think that these pupil/teacher crushes are unhealthy and should be discouraged. I was doing Deirdre a favour.)

We were going to history next. I was sure Deirdre was developing a thing for Mr Dow as well. The school's educational psychologist was going to be kept busy with her.

On the way we passed a milling crowd of ex-St Ann's.

"We're going to the art room to make our tee-shirts," they jeered as we hastily stuffed our airtex tops

into our bags. "*We* won't be wearing those stupid
things when *we* do PE. This the right way?" they asked
as they turned into the corridor.

"Yes," we called back cheerily as they surged down
the passageway to the boys' changing-rooms.

The history classroom was along the corridor, across
the other side of the school quad and up one flight of
stairs. Whoever had drawn up the timetable had taken
a course in masochism, not logistics. The school was a
basic square built around a quadrangle on two levels,
with an admin block and various bits and pieces added
on. Our timetable was designed so that as each subject
followed the other the only prerequisite appeared to be
that the classrooms would be as far distant from each
other, and as complicated to reach as possible.

12

"Is that mine?" Mr Dow our history teacher inspected the pristine white, starched and ironed handkerchief which Deirdre Glissop had presented him with.

"Yeth sir," Deirdre had developed a lisp overnight. "My mummy washed and prethed it for you and said to thank you."

Mr Dow blew his nose on it, polished his glasses and stuffed it in his pocket.

"Right, settle down you lot." He started to read from a sheet of paper. "Heritage Centre visit for first year pupils." He looked at the date on his watch. "That's this afternoon in fact. Assemble main gate at two p.m." He then went on to explain in words of one syllable how to find the main gate.

An outing with Mr Dow, I thought, this should be fun.

"And the other teacher present will be ..." he checked his list, "Mr Brown."

The class sighed.

"For goodness sake be on time," Mr Dow pleaded. "I don't want any delays."

"It's like being in primary again," I said to Jamie as we marched out and down the main road towards the town.

He made a face as we passed our entrance in the hedge. I half expected him to disappear again but Mr Brown was riding shotgun in the rear and Jamie was keeping a wary eye on him. Poor Deirdre had made a fatal mistake in trying to suck up to him earlier. She had shown him how neatly she had covered her books with sturdy brown paper and on the front the little

adhesive stickers her parents had given her with their
family name and address. "Very nice, dear," he had
said shortly. Then she had asked him how we were getting to the Heritage Centre. He had snorted and said
unless she had made a previous arrangement to be
flown there by the RAF in a helicopter she was walking
like everybody else. I heard him muttering to himself
as she went off. "Scarcely out of nappies, some of
them."

We had divided into two groups. Mr Dow had got most
of the St Ann's intake. Mr Brown was with the assorted
Spindle Streeters and me.

The Heritage Centre was a fairly recent addition to
the town and was always full of American and
Australian tourists, trying to trace their Scottish ances-
try. We marched through the park. The rowan berries
were out on the trees and the sky was clear and blue as
the weather hesitated before committing itself to
autumn. There was a huge maple tree just outside the
entrance with deep yellow leaves. Mr Brown lined us all
up.

"Listen to me very carefully indeed," he ordered
grimly. "You will go in here and you will behave perfectly. There will be *no* messing about or disruptive
behaviour from any of you. A member of staff will be
waiting to show you around. I will collect you later in
the entrance hall." He surveyed us and shook his head.
"Scruffy lot. There are frequently important visitors
from overseas here. So while you are in there just pretend I am not with you. I do not know you.
Understand?"

We all nodded furiously and filed inside.

The place was busy with staff and visitors thronging
round the hallway and shop. Mr Dow's group was taken
at once while we milled around waiting. Shortly after, a

guide came forward to greet us and Mr Brown made to move off.

Then Jamie served his ace. Right down the centre line — you could almost see the puff of chalk dust. He addressed Mr Brown directly.

"*Dad*", he said in a loud voice. "I am going to be sick."

There was total silence.

"Da-aaad," Jamie whined, wiping his nose noisily with the back of his sleeve, "I am going to be *sick*."

A wordless message flashed between the Spindle Streeters.

"Daddy," this little red-haired girl, who to my certain knowledge hadn't opened her mouth in any class before, tugged Mr Brown's sleeve. "Daddy," she said, "can I have an ice cream? Please," she pleaded as he tried to shake her off, "pleeeese."

"Heh, Paw," yelled another. "I need a ... you know ... Where do you go here to do a ..." Fortunately the end of the sentence was lost in the rest of the noise.

"Daaaddy, I'm needing too."

"Can I get something out the shop?"

"Look at that nice family. Gee, I just love big old-fashioned families, don't you, honey?" an American voice drawled. "Isn't that little girl real cute?"

"Daddy, can I have money for sweeties? Remember, you promised."

"I want a drink," I said. (I know, I know, it wasn't very inspired but it was the best I could do at a moment's notice.)

The guide launched into her rehearsed speech in a loud voice. She had obviously dealt with hecklers before.

"Welcome to the Heritage Centre," she said, "please follow me to the first level."

We all came together immediately and trotted off dutifully behind her. I didn't dare look back.

13

"Jamie. You are dead meat." I eventually managed, in the local history section, to get close enough to tell him this.

He shrugged. "I don't think so. Pa Broon would have to give the whole class a punny, and then it would be found out what he said to us before we came in here. Anyway, it was worth it, he deserved it."

This was certainly true, deserve it he did. I thought of my parents' reaction to having to sign a punishment exercise on my third day of term, especially as they had not been too chuffed with my first day. I decided to put it out of my mind and concentrate on our guide. She was telling us of the town of yester-year.

"The oldest part of this town is the area where your school is. There was once a medieval castle on that site, the road there follows the lines of a road used by packmen many years ago. The graveyard, although now a mile or two by road from there, also dates from early times. It is, as you can see, fairly close to the castle site as the crow flies. There was once a small river separating the two which has since dried up. The history of the graveyard is very interesting because it is so old. There are a few famous people buried there. It is of value as a social history, there are the graves of the victims of the cholera outbreak in the last century, and you will notice if you read the inscriptions how many children died when they were very young. Lack of medical care and social facilities meant that a lot of young people died before reaching adulthood, sometimes from quite common illnesses."

I thought of Kathleen Campbell and the measles and shivered.

"Of course the thing that interests children nowadays are the stories of the bodysnatchers. You will have all heard of Burke and Hare, the two Edinburgh men who lived last century? They were not content with merely grave-robbing. They began to kill people to supply the medical schools with fresh bodies. We don't think that anyone in these parts resorted to actual murder, but there were bodysnatchers here. The value of a corpse was about £10, a great deal of money in those days. A lookout tower was built in our cemetery so that new graves could be watched over, and a watchman was appointed to guard new graves."

"That's my great-grandad she's talking about," said Jamie.

She unrolled an old map.

"You can see here where the graveyard and the castle site are marked quite clearly."

"I grabbed Jamie's arm.

"Our path," I said. "Let's get closer."

The guide was very pleased at our interest as we leaned over the map.

"Can you see it?" I asked Jamie.

"See what?" asked a familiar voice behind us. It was Mr Brown.

We both tried to merge into the furniture.

"What mischief are you two up to?" he asked.

He studied me carefully. "Did you break your glasses or something?" he asked. "Are you wearing a pair of your father's? Is that why you are peering so closely at this map?"

I had forgotten that I was wearing my Proclaimers glasses. I snatched them off quickly, which was not a good idea. My eyes began to water immediately and everything was a blur.

To be strictly honest, I had needed glasses for a little time before I had actually got them. When I was in primary school my mother had suspected that perhaps my eyesight was not as it should be. I think the final straw came for her on the night of the primary Christmas play, when in the stable, I picked up one of the cardboard sheep and said slowly and reverently, "Behold the Holy Infant." It was shortly after that when she took me to an optician to have my eyes tested.

I put my glasses on again.

"These are my proper glasses," I said indignantly. "I have several different pairs. We *are* actually looking for something — a right of way which belongs to us." I was so annoyed that I had blurted out what we were looking for.

"A right of way?" he said. "As far as I know Ordnance Survey maps in Scotland do not disclose the existence of rights of way. Is that correct?" he asked the guide.

"Yes," she said, "but there is a district guide to rights of way in this area. Hold on."

She brought it out and Jamie and I looked carefully. Nothing.

"Well, that's that then," Jamie said miserably.

"Would you two like to tell 'Daddy' what is going on?" asked Mr Brown.

We both grimaced. I could hardly believe he was taking the joke which had been played on his so well. It wasn't possible that he had a sense of humour.

I think that Jamie was so relieved not to be told off that he explained about the lane and the field and the farmer putting up fences. He edited the bullfight episode.

Mr Brown seemed very interested. He consulted with the Heritage guide for a few minutes.

"Our visit here is nearly over," he said. "However, I am a member of the local community council, and if you like I'll take this up with them. It is important that paths such as this are not lost to the public."

I don't remember actually agreeing that he would help us, but then, as I told my parents later, I suppose that I didn't actually *disagree*. I didn't honestly think that he would appear later at my front door to speak to them, nearly giving them, and me, heart failure.

14

"Don't you have any homework tonight?" My mother had stopped me with this ancient chestnut as I was preparing to leave the house that evening. Jamie had suggested I might want to come over and plan a bull disposal unit.

I hopped from one foot to the other. I was already late.

"Done it."

"Well, you can't have done it very neatly. You have only been in your room five minutes. Now I have warned you, Mary, you have to have a bit more application in secondary school. I see it all from the other side of the fence, children with real potential getting nowhere. If you don't start a study habit at once you will be left behind."

She was going into her "a good education will serve you the rest of your life" routine. I glanced at my watch.

"Look, could you fast forward this next bit? I am in a bit of a hurry."

I thought I had put my request quite politely but with parents you never can tell. It was another twenty minutes before I got away. And I had to explain exactly where I was going, and when I would be back. I was out of breath by the time I reached the cottage. Jamie let me in. His mother was remoulding some of her sculpture with an oxyacetylene torch.

"She looks dangerous," I said to Jamie. "shouldn't she be outside?"

"She says she gets good vibrations from the cottage, it being so old and all. She's getting more careful now.

It must be at least a month since she has set anything on fire."

"That would be a good bull deterrent," I said.

"I don't want to hurt the beast, I'd rather turn it on the farmer."

We both clowned about with imaginary flame-throwers. Jamie's mother ignored us. I could just imagine mine if I brought a friend home and we jumped all over her Sanderson carpets and Habitat furniture. She never allowed me any free expression. She was very cutting to me about my part in the Christmas pageant. I must admit I did ad lib slightly at one bit. Well, apart from the fact that I was not going to allow the teacher's pet, Jean Robertson, who was playing the part of the innkeeper's wife, to upstage me, there was a legitimate reason for my short impromptu speech. I was only trying to draw attention away from the spectacle of Mrs Cult, the drama teacher, crawling on her hands and knees across the stage with a shovel, attempting to scoop up half a hundredweight of donkey dung.

"Got you!" I shouted at Jamie.

He rolled on to the floor trying to douse the fire in his clothes.

"What's that?" I said.

By the sound of the banging on the front door the person there had obviously been trying to make themselves heard for some time.

"Okay, okay. I'm coming," said Jamie. He got up from the rug and opened the door. Mr Brown stood there. He had some papers in his hand.

He looked past us at the chaos and the sculptor in action.

"Is there anyone responsible at home?" he asked.

"Only my mum," said Jamie.

Jamie's mum came over.

"Can I help you?" she asked sweetly.

She was dressed in her bottling plant working clothes, i.e. old jumper and jeans. Also her hair was tousled and there were dirty streaks on her face.

Mr Brown fell for her. Later Jamie disagreed with me, but as a woman, and a sensitive human being, I *knew*. You could almost hear the sound as he crashed.

"It's Jamie's mother I'm looking for," he said.

"Yes, that's me."

"Really, you look far too young."

("Pathetic," I thought.)

She smiled at him.

"It's about the right of way. I am on the local community council and I think I may have some information which could help. We have dealt with a few cases previous to this one. If you can make a good argument the district council are very supportive."

"I am so sorry," said Jamie's mum. "I haven't had time to read the book Jamie brought home. I was making some alterations to this."

"What is it you are working on?" Mr Brown asked.

"It is an alternative to depressing traditional tombstones. Tell me your first impressions. Truthfully."

"I think it's lovely," he said.

I noticed he was still gazing at Jamie's mum and not the sculpture.

"Oh," she said in a delighted voice. "to be absolutely honest nobody has ever said that before. Has anyone close to you died recently?" she added.

"Shall we discuss the right of way?" asked Mr Brown. He waved his leaflets around. "There is some useful information here."

He then outlined all the points which we could put forward to support our case.

"Rights of way have to be from one public place to another. That is fine from the School Road side, because that is a public road, albeit accessed through a hedge. The drawback is that the public access to the graveyard is here, on the west well, and *not* your son's unofficial entrance. Anyway, I'll telephone the district council offices and ask to talk to their planning officer."

"I wonder ..." said Jamie's mum. "I always had the impression that there had been an ancient track there. A kind of shortcut to the graveyard. Maybe burial parties coming from the older part of the town." She had started to rummage in a cupboard built in at the side of the range. "There might be something in here among our family papers."

15

Jamie's mum dragged an old tin trunk out of the cupboard.

"Here, let me help you." Mr Brown sprang gallantly to her aid. He grabbed her oxyacetylene torch, which had been on the point of igniting the trunk, the papers in it, and possibly the whole house, and carefully extinguished it.

"Ooops," she said. "Thanks."

"Make us some coffee," said Mr Brown to Jamie.

Jamie grimaced behind his back but I noticed that he put the kettle on quickly and set out some mugs.

"This is a beautiful house," said Mr Brown, "and in such good condition. When does it date from?"

"My great-grandfather built it in the 1800s," said Jamie's mother. "He was appointed gravekeeper. He used to watch for bodysnatchers. He kept diaries and papers dating from much earlier. I think his father and grandfather were undertakers, or whatever those people were called at that time. It is a sort of family tradition."

"Oh, well, at least young Jamie will not be out of a job when he leaves school. There are always plenty of customers in this line of work," said Mr Brown. He warmed his hands at the range. "This log fire is a rare treat."

"Yes," said Jamie's mum. "We collect blown branches and use peat in the winter. Apple tree smells the best." She looked around her. "The major drawback is that it is so small." She and Jamie exchanged glances. She began to take old photographs and letters out of the trunk.

"Oh, look," she said. "Jamie! Here you are in your pram."

Mr Brown and I peered at a red-faced infant with a huge dummy stuck in its mouth.

"You were a lovely baby," sighed Jamie's mum.

"Only a mother could say that," muttered Mr Brown.

"And here's another, of you in your wee bath."

Jamie snatched the photograph from his mother's hand before anyone could see it and stuffed it in his pocket.

"Coffee's ready," he said.

At this point someone knocked very briskly on the cottage door. Jamie opened it to reveal my parents. That was all I needed. I had hoped to keep them under wraps until our friendship was more securely established. He invited them in.

"We came to collect Mary," said my mother.

"And to see if we could be of any help," added my father. "Your teacher, Mr Brown, had called on us earlier on, to get some more information on your right of way, and we told him you were here."

"I didn't realize it was an actual right of way which you were talking about last night," said my mother to me reproachfully. "I thought it was a project."

"It *is* a project," I said.

"Yes, but I thought it was a *school* project, dear. You know," she addressed Mr Brown, "we even went down to the library the other night to do some research on it."

"Very commendable," he murmured.

"Speaking as teachers ourselves," said my father (I groaned), "we are glad to see the youngsters interesting themselves in this sort of thing."

"Do sit down and have some coffee," said Jamie's mother.

My mother hesitated before taking a place on the

couch. It was an ancient settee with sagging springs
and had an old travelling rug slung over it. I don't
think it was its age or condition which made her hesi-
tate, it was the books, magazines, toys et cetera which
she had to negotiate before she could find a space. She
eventually picked up Jamie's football and sat down
with it on her lap. She sipped her coffee nervously and
looked about her. It was obviously a deep culture shock
to my mother that not everyone lived in a wall-to-wall
carpeted, fitted-kitchen environment.

They all introduced themselves. My mother gave
Jamie a penetrating look.

"So this is your new friend, Mary," she said slowly.

Jamie rattled around with coffee and a plate of biscuits but it was no good. You could tell she had assessed
him at once as "unsuitable."

Mr Brown explained what they were doing. He
began to examine papers in the trunk.

"You know, these are very interesting," he said.
"Apart from anything to do with the right of way, some
of these documents are of great historical value. The
Heritage Centre would probably appreciate a look at
them and want to make copies if possible. A lot of this
tells the history of the town, which I am quite interested in, and as far as I know there is no other original
source for this material."

He spread an old map out on the rug.

"This shows the old castle site behind where the
school is now. It was originally based on a Roman fort,
you know. The fort was one of the ones on the
Antonine Wall. There have been excavations done
there in the past but nothing very much has been
found. People used to use it as a kind of quarry and
take away the stones for building walls et cetera round
about here. The castle must have been less of a ruin

then than it is now. No path marked though, I'm
afraid."

He studied the map for a few more minutes.

"There is a river clearly marked but I don't see any
bridge. That means the only way to walk from the castle to the graveyard would be by the long route, the
way the main road is today. So ..." he folded up the map
slowly, "it would appear that there is no right of way."

16

We all went outside. It was a quiet evening with a sharp clear moon. Despite myself, I was beginning to see something attractive in graveyards. Regular lines, neatly trimmed pathways, imposing tombstones.

Mr Brown spoke to my parents before we drove away.

"I was planning to go to the Heritage Centre tomorrow," he said. "You're welcome to come. We could plough our way through the local history material and see if we come up with anything."

My parents thought that this was a wonderful way to spend a Saturday afternoon. They nodded agreement.

"Also," Mr Brown went on, "I'm sure there must be some flora down there worth preserving. I could contact our local wildlife group. There should be interesting plants in that field, especially if it has been undisturbed for a number of years." He glanced at Jamie. "Well, relatively undisturbed," he added.

I pulled Jamie aside.

"Is that or is that not typical of adults?" I said. "It is *our* project and *our* right of way, and do they include us? They do not!"

"Are you telling me that you actually *want* to spend a Saturday afternoon at the Heritage Centre?" asked Jamie.

"Well, no ..." I replied. "What do you normally do on a Saturday, anyway?"

He hesitated for a second.

"I visit my grandad," he said. "D'you want to come?"

On Saturday morning we went to visit Jamie's grandad.

He was in sheltered accommodation known as "Restful Retirements Inc." in the centre of the town.

"I take him out every week," said Jamie as we went in the main door. "We call it 'The Great Escape.'"

"Why did he come in here if he doesn't like it?" I asked.

"He's dead old," said Jamie, "and when my mum and dad split up we had to sell our house, so grandad James gave mum his cottage and came in here."

His room was third along the bottom corridor.

"You get the stuff past the matron?" the old man hissed as soon as Jamie entered his room.

"Yeh," said Jamie at once, and produced a brown paper bag from under his jerkin.

"Want some?" grandad offered me.

My mind boggled. This was what I had been warned against all my life and now it was actually happening to *me*. What were they pushing? Magic mushrooms? LSD?

"*Say No!*" Nancy Reagan had exhorted every kid in America.

"What kind of stuff would that be, exactly?" I enquired tentatively.

Jamie's grandad was fumbling with the bag.

"What is it this week, Jamie?"

"Dolly mixtures," said Jamie. "He's not allowed sweets," he said to me, as he tucked the rug round his grandad's knees and turned the wheelchair towards the door.

"If he's not allowed sweets why are you giving them to him?" I whispered as we trundled along the corridor.

"He's not allowed his beer, or to smoke his pipe, and he's ninety-two years old for heaven's sake." Jamie banged the wheelchair through the doors and down the path outside towards the park. "And it's only once a week, so shut up."

I did.

"Grandad," said Jamie as we reached the pond, "we've got a problem."

There was a sharp plop and a swan which had been gracefully preening moved off swiftly into the middle of the lake.

"What was that?" I asked as another small object zipped into the water. They were definitely coming from the direction of the wheelchair.

"Grandad doesn't like the jelly ones," said Jamie casually. "He sucks the sugar off them and then fires them in the pond. His aim is quite good, actually."

I couldn't believe it. Ninety-two years old and no respect for wild creatures.

Jamie outlined the right of way drama, playing up to a ridiculous extent his part in stopping the bull. Frankly I was aghast at his exaggeration. You'd have thought that he personally had wrestled that bull to its knees.

I opened my mouth to interrupt. Then I noticed that Grandad James was gazing at Jamie with adoration, following his every word and obviously thrilled with the story. I closed my mouth.

"So what are we going to do about it?" he asked.

Jamie shrugged his shoulders.

"I don't know," he said, producing a rather crumpled object from his pocket. "I brought my right of way booklet. D'ye want to look at it?"

I was going to point out that it was *my* right of way booklet and that I was sure in the by-laws printed on the inside front cover there was something relating to the penalties for the misuse of library books. But I didn't.

"You know," said Jamie's grandad as he began to flick through the book, "working outdoors all my life I did know something of the country code. There are old routes like drove roads when taking cattle to market that are historic rights of way."

He found a page in the book.

"Here is the one that I'm thinking of. Routes taken by burial parties on their way to graveyards."

"Yeh, mum mentioned that last night, but when we checked the old maps in the trunk there was nothing marked."

"As I recall," said Jamie's grandad, "you have a lot of stuff pinned up in your room. Now that map is the oldest one I had."

"I'll run back and get it," said Jamie. "Look after grandad," he shouted at me, and before I could protest he was off.

"Push me round the pond, little girl," commanded Grandad James.

(*Little Girl?*) It was only that I had been brought up to be polite to the elderly that prevented me from making a suitable reply. As we got nearer to the water I realized that his object was not to appreciate nature but to increase his accuracy in maiming the wildlife. I prayed that Jamie would run fast.

17

The relief of Mafeking was nothing to the enthusiastic welcome I gave Jamie on his return. People were beginning to stare, as his tiny pellets plopped into the water. Mothers were drawing young children closer beside them and away from us.

We spread the ancient map across the old man's lap, and leaned over the yellowed and cracked parchment.

"I can't read it," said Jamie. "Wait." He pulled a magnifying glass out of his pocket. "I thought we might need this."

It was strange to read this map, out in the bright sunlight with the old gravekeeper. To see twentieth-century people with their plastic and polythene, their synthetic laminate coffins and piped music in crematoriums, trying to trace a path trodden in past centuries by Jamie's ancestors on their solemn way to bury their dead.

"There is the river," said Jamie, "and it is running right across the back access to that field and the graveyard stile."

"Yes, I'm sure I remember that from when I was small," said Grandad James, "though it had almost dried up by then."

"Well, it must have been much larger long ago. It says here 'liable to flooding.'"

Jamie pointed to some wavy lines on the map. "See?"

"Yes, but the procession to the grave wouldn't be coming by that particular route," argued Jamie's grandad. "They would be coming from the direction of the church."

He traced a line with his finger.

"The old church was about here."

"The bridge for crossing is much further down the river," said Jamie. "We looked at it last night. It is nearer to the present entrance to the graveyard."

"They would never walk all that way round," insisted Grandad James. "There must be something we are missing."

Jamie's grandad took the magnifying glass from Jamie's hand. He peered at the map carefully. After a moment he looked up and smiled.

"There is a ford marked," he said quietly, "just above your entrance in the hedge and inside the farm land."

His hand, brown-spotted with age like the map, trembled slightly.

"You can just make out some writing if you study it closely. It says, 'Here is placed The Coffin Stone.'"

He laid down the magnifying glass. "The *ford* is where the burial parties would cross and the bearers would rest the coffin on a stone in the middle of the stream!"

"Are you sure?" asked Jamie.

"There is another stone like that which is quite famous," said Grandad James. "It is called the Carrick Stone and it is in Cumbernauld. It was an ancient Roman 'Ara' or altar and it was used as a resting-place for coffins being taken to the graveyard there."

"So it *is* legit," said Jamie. "There *is* an ancient right of way."

He threw his arms round his grandad's neck and hugged him. So did I. (Well, it was quite an emotional moment and I got caught up in the spirit of the thing.) Jamie's grandad didn't seem to mind.

"Is this enough proof?" asked Jamie.

"Don't know," said Grandad James as he spat another denuded jelly tot at the ducks in the pond. "It should be enough to make some kind of case." He consulted his pocket watch.

"Oh, sorry grandad," said Jamie quickly, and turned the wheelchair towards the home. "The wrestling is on soon," he explained to me, "and I have to get there early to get the best seat in the lounge."

"We're going to have to move fast," said Jamie as he walked back down the town. "The farmer told mum that he was going ahead with his plans to modernize and upgrade the land. He said he had done a lot of work already, and had more to do, infilling holes and ditches, some of the perimeter was in a dreadful state, he said, and no one was going to stop him now."

"What kind of moves were you thinking of?" I asked nervously.

"I have an idea," said Jamie.

I should have known better than to ask. As he started to tell me what his "idea" was I thought of previously arranged engagements for Saturday which might just have happened to have slipped my mind: hospital visiting, dental appointments, choir practice, anything ...

"Actually go up there?" I repeated. "To the farm? Why?"

"We might find a clue," said Jamie, "some vital piece of evidence." There was a gleam of excitement in his eye. "What do you say?" he said.

What could I say?

18

"Definitely not, Jamie," I said. "No way. I am not going in there. Wild horses wouldn't drag me."

Jamie and I had started at the outside edge of the farmer's "bull field" walking along the gully, away from our lane and the graveyard. We could see the bull grazing at the far end. Jamie stopped for a minute and peered through the fence.

"What are you doing?" I asked.

"I thought there might be bits of my body stunner lying about and you could distract the bull while I nipped in and got them."

It was my turn to grab him by the collar and pull him firmly away.

We moved deeper into enemy territory.

We were heading towards the ruins of the town's medieval castle situated somewhere behind our secondary school. Jamie kept consulting his map which he had copied from the one in his house and stopping to pick up various stones and items he put in his rucksack.

"Evidence," he said mysteriously, when I asked him why.

Up till now we had been on what appeared to be common land. The dried-up river bed was full of boulders and holes and quite difficult to clamber along. The going was rough and I had already snagged my sweatshirt twice before we came on a roughly erected barrier which had "DANGER KEEP OUT" painted on it.

It was at this point that I put my foot down.

"No," I repeated firmly. "That is a definite 'No Entry.'"

"This is not his land, it is the boundary line," Jamie said. "He has just put that up recently. He has no right." He squirmed under. "Come on."

"Absolutely not," I said. "He probably bought up all those redundant Berlin Wall guard dogs and he's got them prowling about in there. Anyway, that couldn't have been the path. It's a jungle."

"Of course it is all overgrown *now*," said Jamie, "because it has been allowed to get that way."

He showed me his map again.

"See," he insisted, 'there is a track or a path marked."

There certainly appeared to be a dotted line, coming down from this area.

"I think that is the old coffin path and I am going to find out," said Jamie firmly.

"Well, I'm not."

I turned away ...

It was in a clearing only a hundred yards or so beyond the barrier that we came across the tractor. Jamie grabbed my arm and pulled me behind a bush.

"I am going to reconnoitre," he whispered.

"I'm coming with you," I said.

I wasn't staying there myself. I was sure I could hear the panting and slavering of wild beasts among the undergrowth.

We crept forward. I held firmly onto Jamie's rucksack. If we had to make a run for it, it would be together.

There was no one around. He had probably gone for his lunch. The trailer was filled with stones and rocks and there was some more loaded in the tipper at the top.

"Your mum said he was working on the land, infilling holes and things," I said.

"I'll bet he is going to fill up the whole gully and extend his land right up to the hedge," said Jamie indignantly.

From the farmer's point of view I thought it would seem a perfectly sensible thing to do.

"We are going to have to do something quickly if he is to be stopped," said Jamie.

I didn't enquire as to what he had in mind. Having encountered previously Jamie's regard for the law, I imagined that it would probably be something illegal, like immobilizing the tractor.

"I think we should go back straightaway and report this," I said.

Jamie didn't even bother to reply. He climbed up on the tractor. "He must have taken the keys away with him."

I breathed a sigh of relief.

"What a pity," I said.

Jamie jumped back down.

I grabbed the strap of his rucksack again. I could see the farm buildings through the trees, and was becoming nervous.

"I wonder where he's dumping that lot," Jamie said. "Let's look around here."

He studied the ground.

"There are tracks over this way."

He moved back towards the old river bed.

"Not animal tracks, I hope."

He claimed afterwards that it was my fault as he had turned his head to answer me. Otherwise he would certainly have spotted the gaping hole which appeared at our feet.

I was still clutching at his rucksack, which was why, when the ground at the edge of the hole which the farmer was filling, gave way, both of us fell right in.

19

I suppose Jamie got the worst of it as I actually fell on top of him. We scrambled up. I couldn't see a thing. I must have been hit on the head I thought at once.

"I've gone blind," I shrieked.

"For heaven's sake," said Jamie and rammed my glasses back on my face.

"Oh."

I peered out from one cracked lens. My sweatshirt was now torn and my jeans filthy. I tried not to think on what tonight's inquest at home would be like.

We couldn't get out.

I tried standing on top of Jamie's shoulders but I was unable even to touch the top edge of the hole into which we had fallen. It had a fairly narrow entrance but widened out as it deepened and the sides were too far apart to chimney our way up.

Jamie looked up. The sky was a long way off.

"This is a very deep hole," he said eventually.

There was one huge stone just below the opening. It crossed my mind that had we hit that when we landed then we would have had more than a few scrapes and bruises. We tried piling other rocks which were lying about on top of this, but it was no good, they kept falling off and it didn't reach half high enough anyway.

We were trapped!

"This reminds me of something which happened in our primary school Christmas pageant," I said.

"Shut up about your sodding Christmas pageant," said Jamie roughly.

I was quite offended. I had only wanted to keep our minds off the situation. After all, that was what people in the air-raid shelters had done and it had seen them through the war. I hesitated about suggesting a sing-song to Jamie. He didn't seem very receptive.

"Okay, smarty," I said. "What do you suggest? Haven't you got anything useful in that rucksack? An extending ladder, for instance."

He searched in his bag. Apart from a load of old stones and other bits of rubbish there was nothing of use.

"You should have been properly prepared," I said, "with a rope or something."

"If you hadn't been nattering on about wild animals this wouldn't have happened. Here."

He offered me a piece of Highland toffee. I thought of my braces and declined. I didn't want to have my mouth permanently glued together. Then he found his torch and shone it round about us. I wish he hadn't bothered. A thousand earwigs and beetles materialized at my feet and scuttled into the darkness. I shuddered.

"Don't tell me you're scared of beetles," said Jamie scornfully.

"No," I lied. Well, it was more than just beetles. The list included spiders, mice, slugs and various flying insects. I also felt that I was beginning to develop slight claustrophobic tendencies. I didn't want him to think he was cooped up with a total neurotic and panic.

"What's that over there?" I asked nervously.

There was a heavy piece of metal lying in one corner. We examined it.

"I think it's a mortsafe," said Jamie. "It was an iron frame which they used to clamp round coffins before burying them, and then after a few weeks they opened the grave and took them away. They were so heavy that it prevented bodysnatching. I wonder why it's here?"

He examined some broken pieces of stone.

"There is lettering and signs on these. I think these are bits of mortslabs. This pit must have been used as a dumping ground by previous farmers." He shone his torch right into the corner. It was at this point I saw the bones.

I must admit that a tiny whimper escaped my lips at this moment. Beetles and spiders were bad enough, but at least they were alive.

"These are bones," said Jamie with real enthusiasm in his voice.

He obviously had inherited ghoulish tendencies from his mother's side of his family. "Blood will out" as my father always says. Jamie was picking up these human remains and examining them more carefully. Perhaps his criminal inclinations came from his father. He hadn't mentioned him apart from saying to Mr Brown that he hadn't got one. Perhaps the absent dad was a lifer on the Isle of Wight. What a genetic combination this child had. Great things lay ahead for him. He would probably become the next prime minister.

"I wonder how old these are," said Jamie.

"I don't think we should touch them at all," I said edging away. "Goodness knows whose bones they are."

My mind was not allowed to dwell on this for very long as Jamie suddenly said, "It's gone very dark."

He went and looked at the opening in the roof.

"Oh, my God!" he said.

I rushed over and saw what was blocking the light. The farmer had returned and we had been so busy with our discoveries that we had not heard the approach of the tractor. The light to our hole was being blocked by the tipper which was that very moment poised to drop tons of rocks and stones on top of us.

You must understand that I am normally a very

calm and resourceful person, but I had had a trying
afternoon. What with beetles and bodies it became all
too much for me and I'm afraid I let go. I did the only
thing a woman could do in those circumstances.

I screamed.

20

... and screamed, and screamed.

Jamie clamped his hand over my mouth.

"*Shut up!*" he yelled. "Listen."

We both listened.

"All I am asking," said the distinctive voice of Mr Brown, our teacher, "is for you to delay two minutes before dumping those rocks."

"No," said the farmer.

"Look," said Mr Brown in a very patient voice (which must have been a real effort for him), "I think you may have gathered up some very important archaeological pieces there and I would welcome the chance to have a quick look and pick out anything of interest from the tipper before you dump them down there."

"No," said the farmer.

"I can see from here," said Mr Brown desperately, "there is a stone there which is a very interesting example of cross hatching. It was how the Romans prepared stones for the Antonine Wall."

"No," said the farmer.

"Have you no sense of history, man?" shouted Mr Brown, now losing his temper.

The farmer obviously hadn't. "Get out of my way," he said, "or I'll run you down."

Jamie and I looked at each other.

We both screamed.

After a few moments, as death had not descended from the sky, we stopped. We could hear Mr Brown pleading with the farmer, and the farmer appeared to be changing his mind.

"Well, I suppose the light's nearly gone anyway ... Right, you can take a look tomorrow ..."

And to our absolute dismay we heard their voices fading in the distance. Jamie and I didn't say anything for a moment or two.

"You don't have a torch?" I asked. My voice wavered slightly. The prospect of spending a night in a dark hole with scurrying creatures was beginning to upset me.

"Look," said Jamie seriously. "We have to get out of here now. This hole is so deep they couldn't hear us yelling. He might come back in the morning and start the tractor and just dump that load down here ..." He trailed off.

His voice sounded a bit wavery.

"What if we dragged that iron thing over and propped it against the big stone?" I suggested.

Jamie went over and heaved at the end of the mort-safe.

"I see what you're getting at. We could use it as a kind of ramp to reach the top."

We both put our fingers under the edge and tried to pull.

It seemed to take us hours. As a device to lay on top of graves to stop bodysnatching it must have been super-efficient. We eventually managed to bring it to rest leaning against the stone and sticking up towards the mouth of the hole.

Jamie climbed up to have a look. It was still quite far short of the top. He was silhouetted against the clear night sky.

I couldn't help noticing that the Great Bear constellation was beginning to shine out in the gathering darkness.

"Oh, look!" I cried out. "The Great Bear!" (Well, I

thought he might want to observe it. He would have a particularly good view from his position. Honestly, I didn't mean to startle him.)

I won't tell you what he said as he slithered back down and crashed at the bottom. Really! I'm quite sure they never used language like that even in the trenches.

We had a quick discussion and decided that Jamie would climb back up. I would climb up after and try to stand on his shoulders (me being the lighter) and heave myself towards the edge and freedom.

When I say *we* decided, I actually mean Jamie, but I suppose there wasn't much choice. I kept telling myself this as I nervously climbed onto his shoulders. It was just as well I couldn't see down. I grabbed a handful of his hair to steady myself, stood up and then launched my body towards the rim.

At the last second he had (quite nobly, I will admit) let go his hold to give me a massive punt. This resulted in him falling off the mortsafe with extensive bruising but also had the effect of landing me face down in the field above.

My glasses smashed immediately, of course. I got up and groped around a bit, being extremely careful to stay well back from the edge.

"I'll be back soon," I shouted and then, pointing myself in what I hoped was the direction of the graveyard, I started to run.

21

I suppose it wouldn't have bothered Jamie at all, being out alone, after dark, among strange bushes and trees. For myself, I had to slow down quite soon. Apart from my limited vision, I found that my energy was gone and being walloped in the face by stray branches didn't help.

Another thought which had crossed my mind was also causing me to reduce speed. What was I going to tell my parents? I had, without actually saying in so many words, indicated that I would do some historical research with Jamie in the afternoon, and then probably meet them later in the Heritage Centre. The Heritage Centre would be long closed. They had probably contacted Interpol by now.

I decided to go to the cottage first. It was quicker. Maybe I could persuade Jamie's mum to take me home and surely her presence would forestall any actual physical violence by my parents towards me.

I reached the graveyard.

Now, as I have explained to you before, I knew that Jamie and I were destined for friendship, twin souls almost. However, that did not mean that we were completely in tune in our outlook. Jamie and graveyards had something in common. To me a graveyard at night was not a fun place to be. All warnings about strangers, and the police safety leaflets *re* Out Late Walking Alone — Don't, were starting to run in my brain.

I glanced about cautiously as I entered the cemetery gate. Jamie's house was a little way in by the west wall. I took the turn down the first path.

He nearly got me. I was busy looking from side to side when suddenly, directly in front of me, was an attacker! Stretched forward, arm upraised. I identified it immediately — the classic posture of combat. Well, I was prepared. Not for nothing had I practised in PE. Mrs Pollock would be proud of me. I took my position and went into action. Textbook precision. Grab, Bend, Twist. And she was right, Mrs Pollock. It *did* produce severe pain. I was on the ground howling and yelling when Mr Brown, my parents, and Jamie's mum ran up.

"Where have you been? We've been so worried about you, darling." said my mum and burst into tears.

"Are you all right?" asked my dad and patted my head.

"What the hell have you done to that stone angel?" asked Mr Brown, picking up the broken pieces of a Victorian monument.

As I was sobbing at this point — quite genuinely — it didn't take much to keep it up for a little while longer. Just to tide me over the awkward part. The bit involving the investigation as to where we went after visiting Grandad James and why we didn't tell anyone where we were going, and the state of my clothes, explain one broken tombstone, and "Where were my glasses anyway?"

"Come and have some hot tea," suggested Jamie's mum. I allowed myself to be helped back to the cottage, limping slightly (when the chips are down go for the sympathy vote).

The police were at Jamie's house. They seemed mildly disappointed that they had to cancel their plans to drag the canal. They had been searching for us since dusk when neither of us had returned home.

They had questioned Grandad James because he

had been the last to see us. Jamie's mother told us later that grandad had thought it was something to do with the sweets that Jamie brought him and had refused to co-operate.

I was comfortably seated on the couch with the rug tucked snugly around me and a cup of hot cocoa in my hands. I could feel my eyelids drooping. It would be very nice just to drift off to sleep, I thought.

"Excuse me," said Jamie's mum, after the fuss had stopped.

I smiled at her sweetly.

"Where is Jamie, now, exactly?"

I squealed and dropped my mug.

The birds were chirruping their little heads off in the trees around the field as I led the procession back towards the hole where Jamie was trapped. I didn't realize time could pass so quickly, a nice clear dawn was lightening the sky when we reached the gully.

Did you know that farmers get up very early in the morning? I hadn't appreciated just how early until then. It must be something to do with mucking out byres or milking things. Anyway, there was our farmer leaning up against his tractor whistling, and even I with my defective sight could see quite clearly that the hopper was empty.

I raced across to him. My heart was thumping in my ears. "Where are the stones and rocks that were in this last night?" I screeched.

"I dumped them," he said.

My world turned dim around the edges. I felt as though I was going to be sick.

"Where did you dump them?" asked Mr Brown, who had been close behind me.

The farmer wiped his hands casually on an oily rag.

"Over there," he pointed to a corner of the field.

"You said you wanted a look at them. You'd better be quick though. I haven't got all day."

You know, they made the most tremendous fuss over Jamie when they eventually got him out of that hole. Not that I cared particularly, but you would have thought he had just swum the Channel or something. Mr Brown practically carried him all the way home. (Obviously trying to impress Jamie's mum.) To protect himself, Jamie had made an improvized air-raid shelter from the mortsafe and slabs, and my dad said that showed what an intelligent and resourceful person he was. Huh!

Mr Brown laughed when we mentioned the human bones and said they would probably be the bones of animals who had got trapped in the pit. We didn't dwell on that one when we thought of what might have happened to us.

22

Obviously there is some reasoned intent in starting a school term midweek, some deep, educationally significant purpose — it might be to let the teachers have time to regroup in preparation for the next onslaught. All I know is we had three days of secondary school experience and then a two-day weekend holiday, which meant that some of us had totally forgotten anything we had learned.

You will not believe this, but some of us had actually forgotten which school we were supposed to attend. Well, one of us at any rate.

My mind was on other things, and I feel that there was some justification. I mean, two pairs of smashed spectacles, a wrecked satchel, plus various items of wearing apparel in less than perfect condition. Also I was trying to recover from a traumatic experience and had to endure on Sunday a whole day of confinement with constant nagging. So as I left the parents' car Monday a.m. I was not concentrating properly.

It was rather embarrassing when I glanced about and realized that I was in the playground of my old primary school. Don't laugh. I didn't actually line up with the primary twos. As soon as I realized my mistake I recovered really quickly. I grabbed this small infant in a brand new outsize blazer and rucksack and kissed the top of its head affectionately.

"Bye!" I carolled and waved gaily. "Just saying goodbye to my little cousin," I explained to the young mums clustered at the school gate.

One of them gave me a hard look, left the group quickly and took the child into the school. The rest edged away slightly.

I was going to be late. The road from the town to the secondary school was now empty. I was going to have to walk in the main gate and down miles of corridors by myself. And what was I going to say when I got there? "Yes, well, I am Wally Number One. I actually went into primary school this morning due to a memory lapse." Senile dementia at twelve? Hardly likely.

It was so awfully difficult. This unmapped minefield that we first years had to find our way through when we start secondary. No Christian ever faced a lion with such trepidation. We made our way very carefully in case we stepped in something nasty. To be the same as everyone else — that was the trick. Not to attract attention to ourselves in any way. Some of us, who thought our blazers looked too new, had smeared earth on the pocket badge to give it that "experienced appearance." Some cringed in corners because they found their second-hand uniform embarrassing. One girl I knew, on her first day, had brought ankle socks, long socks, over-the-knee socks, and two pairs of different coloured tights with her in her rucksack. She got in early, checked what everyone else was wearing, then nipped into the toilets and put on the appropriate gear.

Okay, okay. So I should have been able to make up my own mind. My mother said that too, but I just wanted to be sure. All right?

I ran hard but could hear the school bell when I was still a quarter of a mile away. A "late report" on the second week! My secondary career seemed to be squaring up to be even more fraught than the primary.

Someone fell into step beside me. A third year I guessed.

"Sell you a surgery card for a pound," he offered.

"Pardon?"

"A clinic surgery card." He showed me a blank appointment card for the local clinic.

I examined it carefully. "Is this a real surgery card?" I asked.

"Of course it is," he said indignantly. "What do you take me for? Dishonest? I'm straight down the line, not like some. Look," he explained, "you just write in an appointment when you're late, or when you want to skive off. Show it to the office staff and they'll give you a 'permission slip' instead of a 'late report.' A pound," he repeated.

"You're kidding!" I said. I couldn't believe it. I was completely taken aback. Astounded.

I'd heard the going rate was 75p.

Please don't get the wrong impression. I am not normally a moral coward. I can speak out when required. (The case of the Christmas panto postmortem in primary school was an exception. I may have exaggerated slightly the stomach cramps which required me to be taken to casualty in an ambulance with suspected appendicitis. I just felt at the time it would be better for Mrs Cult's sake *not* to dwell on what went wrong. An investigation like that never does any good anyway, and she was becoming quite distressed as the head read out the list of incidents.)

However, I checked my timetable, and guess who I was getting first block? I was going to look a right twit coming in late and I was sure that Pa Broon wouldn't take a "slept in, sir" as an excuse. He probably knew my parents dropped me at the edge of town and no way was I going to admit to going to the primary by mistake. How else could I explain being late?

I parted with the readies. Mistake number one.

Mr Brown examined my permission slip.

"Okay. Sit down, Mary."

He went on with the lesson. I breathed normally again. I had got away with it. Mistake number two.

As we filed out after class he called me back. "May I see your appointment card, please?" he asked sweetly.

Did any undercover agent having her papers examined by the Gestapo feel so nervous? My hand trembled, but then it might under normal circumstances. After all, for all he knew I could be suffering from some rare affliction which caused beetroot-coloured flushes and palsy.

He turned it over slowly.

"It's good," he said, "it's very good. Almost perfect in fact. I am glad to see the third year are mastering their printing techniques so well. As you are obviously unaware, a section of third year publish a scurrilous rag for which they are allowed the use of the print room. They do sometimes attempt to go into business for themselves. One should admire their entrepreneurial skills, I suppose. A product of Thatcherism — in some cases private enterprise is not all that far divorced from graft."

He looked at me severely. "Do you have a problem?" he asked.

I shook my head.

"What is the reason for this?" He waved the appointment card under my nose.

"I just didn't want to have to explain why I was late," I mumbled.

"Why *were* you late?"

I told him.

"Why did you not tell me that in the first place?" he asked. He held up his hand. "No, don't bother to answer," he said. "You spend the first weeks of secondary school trying desperately not to do anything which might connect you with primary school. I can see that this would have been a catastrophe for you, Mary."

He studied the card and then me and then the card again. "You know I should really put you on the proper disciplinary procedure for this." He paused.

My throat was hard and dry and I could feel tears coming behind my eyelids.

"Let's just forget it," he said. "Run along, Mary."

I ran along.

23

I must admit that my normal cool composure had been upset by this little incident. It seemed so unfair. Just when I thought I was doing so well coping with secondary school, one small mishap had cascaded into what could have been a major disaster. Mr Brown had been very understanding. (Actually, when I thought about it most teachers who dealt with first year pupils were quite considerate. They seemed to appreciate that it was quite a traumatic time.) Mr Brown being kind, however, had had the effect of bringing me close to tears. So I took the opportunity as I passed the girls' toilets of nipping in to try to recover before catching up with my class.

I looked in the mirror. My face was bright purple and blotchy. I started to splash cold water on it.

"Are you all right, Mary?"

I raised my head. It was Jean Robertson, the girl I had always thought of as sucking up to the teacher in primary seven.

"Ummm," I said.

"I saw Pa Broon going on and on at you, so I thought I'd wait behind and see if you were okay."

I hadn't realized that Jean could be so thoughtful.

"I'm fine. No problem ..." I started to say, or rather to lie. Then I thought that this is part of the problem of why going to secondary is such a hassle. We first years don't want to admit to each other that we make mistakes. We'd do anything to avoid getting embarrassed. I took a deep breath.

"Actually," I said, "I'll tell you what happened to me this morning." And I did.

She grinned back.

"I did it on Friday," she said, "went back to the primary, by mistake, I mean. I covered it up by pretending I had wanted to come in and speak to our old primary seven teacher." She paused for a second then added quietly, "See, everyone always thought I was the teacher's pet anyway, so they believed my story."

"But you *were* the teacher's pet." It was out before I could stop myself.

"But I didn't want to be," wailed Jean. 'that teacher had been at school with my mum and she always chose me to run messages, or for good parts in plays or to answer out in class. I hated it."

I dried my face and adjusted my glasses. "Why do we have to suffer things we hate?" I asked her. I pointed to my glasses and opened my mouth to reveal the awful fixed brace.

"They are only temporary," she said encouragingly. "More than half the class have braces in just now. And if you really hate your glasses you can get contacts later, but I think you suit them. Honestly. The way you have different pairs to change with. It makes you a really interesting person, Mary."

Making new friends like Jamie in secondary was all very well I thought as we went along the corridor together chatting, but it was good to get some support from primary school pals.

We caught up with our lot as they all crashed noisily into the library and surged about, not sure whether to sit down or not.

The person behind the desk jumped nervously in the manner of a startled woodland animal. We waited for her to stand up and speak to us. Then we realized that she *was* standing up. She pushed her thick round glasses up her nose. They slid back down again at once.

She cleared her throat nervously. We all relaxed. This one looked like fair game.

"Library instruction," she began, her voice croaking a bit, "is an essential part of your first year curriculum. To find your way around a modern library and avail yourself of its facilities is one of the essential life skills of today."

"Ya, sounds good to me," said Barry Baxter (an ex-St Ann's). He sat down and put his feet up on a chair.

"Yeh, give us the news," said someone else perching on a table.

My new soulmate, Jean, pulled out a half-eaten packet of crisps and offered me some.

It was amazing, I thought. Totally cowed by Mr Brown one minute, we could all play up as soon as we thought we would get away with it.

We should have known better. School librarians who have lasted more than one term have a slightly different approach to young and tender minds than the local children's librarian who takes the toddlers' story-time.

She raced out from behind her desk. I had barely time to check out her style as she went past me, a blur of green and black flowery top, purple leggings and red doc boots.

Jamie happened to be the closest.

"I know all that stuff already," he was saying. "I'll just get a book to read." He wandered across to the paperback rack.

"Oh, no you won't, laddie."

She took Jamie by the ear and led him to a table. (As she had to reach up to do this, I considered it no mean feat.)

She glanced around. In one swift movement she had pulled the chair from under Barry's legs and snatched

Jean's packet of crisps from her hand. The person sitting on the edge of the table slid off quickly.

"*Sit down!*

"*On a chair!*

"*Now!*"

We all sat down very quickly. Some of us even folded our arms. *Behind* our backs.

"Understand this, all of you," the librarian said distinctly. "You have a geography project to do first term for which you will use library resources. This is compulsory. There is no choice about whether you wish to participate in this or not. In order to complete this project you need the resources of this library. If you do not behave properly when you are in the library you will be banned." She paused for dramatic effect. "Then *you* may go and explain to the geography principal and the head teacher why you have been unable to complete your work."

She smiled a cold smile. "Now. Let us begin."

"This is a *Library*.

"It is *not:*

(a) a play area;

(b) a social meeting-place;

(c) a snack bar."

We paid close attention.

24

"Come on!"

I felt Jamie grab my arm and using me as his legionary's shield he started to propel his way forward in the dinner queue.

It was lunchtime and by some strange chance we had once more found ourselves together struggling in the hungry wolf pack.

"Hold on," I said and shook my arm free, "there must be a better way of doing this."

We stood back and surveyed the scrum. Even the most massive prop forward would have had second thoughts faced with that mêlée.

"We'll be hours behind if we don't get in there now," said Jamie. "What's keeping you?"

"I'm thinking."

"Pardon me," said Jamie sarcastically. "You should have put up a notice. 'Genius at Work.'"

He started forward.

"I'm going in," he said. "I'm starving."

"Why do you always have to barge at everything? Sometimes subtlety is better. What we need here is some lateral thinking." I indicated the fifth and sixth years. "Look at them."

Apart from those prefects on dinner duty, who valiantly tried to control the line with wild and useless threats, the majority of the upper school went past the queue through a side door into the dinner hall.

"We can't do that," said Jamie, "it's dead obvious we're first years."

"I know we can't actually do *that*," I said, "but it is an indication that there is more than one way to do something. The most direct approach is not always best." (This was something that my Uncle Harry was always telling me. He had said that he had got out of many a scrape by independent thinking.) I looked about me carefully. "Now, if we went out into the yard and around the outside, we would come in by the delivery door which is always left open at this time for putting the slop bins out later.

"We'll never get away with it," said Jamie.

"Well, we won't if we don't try," I said and turned away.

The yard was empty. We got to the delivery door no problem.

"One at a time," I instructed from the side of my mouth. "Taking it very slowly and casually."

I peeked over the glass panels at the top of the door and held my breath. I waited until the prefect at the top of the line had turned away and moved further down to sort somebody out, then I slid casually inside. I flipped an empty tray into my hand and mingled with the group at the hatch.

"Lamb hotpot, steak pie, veggie burger, baked potato?"

"Yes," said Jamie, who was right behind me.

I chose a baked potato. I waved gaily to Jean, Deirdre, Margritte and the rest who were further down the queue.

"I'm going to enjoy this," I said.

"Eighty pence, love," said the dinner lady.

I put my hand in my pocket and came up with ... fluff. I scrabbled about desperately. Where was my pound coin?

"What's the hold-up?"

The prefect, a sixth year boy, had returned.

"What's your problem?" he demanded. Then he

stared at me suspiciously. "Where did you appear from? I don't remember seeing you here a minute ago."

"I ... I ..." I stammered, "I've lost my dinner money."

"First year?" he demanded.

I nodded. I had just remembered what I had spent my pound dinner money on this morning. "My pal might pay me."

"Who?"

I glanced about. Jamie had dematerialized.

"Look," he took the tray from me and gave me a friendly shove, "go to the back of the queue. If there's any left over at the end you can have a 'free.'"

As I walked away, my cheeks burning, I heard him say to the dinner lady, "Some of these first years are still babies. They need their dinner money pinned to their inside pocket with a safety pin."

Margritte and Deirdre gave my sympathetic smiles as I trailed past them. The dinner ladies gave me sympathetic smiles half an hour later as they piled up my plate with lumps of left-over lamb and a rather dishevelled potato. I staggered weakly to a table in the corner and began to eat.

"What happened to you?"

I looked up as Margritte and Deirdre sat down beside me.

"I ... I had to wait to the end. My dinner money, er ..." It was certainly True Confession time today I thought as I explained this morning's fiasco again.

"Gosh!" said Deirdre in admiration. "Mary, you are so brave, doing something like that."

"It wasn't brave," I said truthfully. "It was actually quite stupid. You don't know where something like that is going to end."

Prophetic words. I was soon to find out.

"We'll wait with you," they said loyally as I shovelled food into my growling stomach. It was just as well they did. I was about to be in immediate need of some major protection.

25

We chatted about our class work and the difficulties in trying to follow a timetable.

"It really is very complicated," complained Deirdre. "I mean, they tell you the classroom number and everything for the subject, but some of the classrooms don't have their numbers on the doors, and I get figures mixed up so easily."

I stared at her. Of course! I had completely forgotten that she had problems with numbers and kept writing them back to front. Instead of enjoying a joke at her expense yesterday, maybe I should have been helping her.

"It's the homework," said Margritte, "If you get English homework on your Wednesday English block is it for the next Wednesday English block, or the next time you get English?"

"We get English every day!" said Deirdre.

"See what I mean?" said Margritte.

We all started to laugh.

Then we stopped.

A large menacing shadow had fallen across my veggie/lamb/hotchpotch.

My glasses had slipped down my face so I did not immediately recognize my enterprising third year friend from this morning. However, he certainly recognized me. And at once gave me the very distinct impression that he had been searching for me for some time, and not for the purpose of enquiring solicitously if I was enjoying my dinner.

He kicked a chair over and leaned across the table. "You grass me up?"

"Ah ..." I gulped. A piece of food went the wrong way.

"You did, didn't you?"

I shook my head desperately.

"I've just had a sticky ten minutes with Pa Broon on the subject of one of these." He waved an appointment card under my nose. "What did you tell him?"

"Nothing," I whispered. "Nothing. He guessed. I mean he seemed to know."

The boy pushed his face close to mine.

"Do you know what we do to sneaks in secondary school?" he asked.

I shook my head. I had stopped eating. Suddenly I was no longer hungry.

"Well, I'm going to tell you. In fact," he came round the table and sat down beside me. He waved the card under my nose, "I think I'll *show* you."

"Why don't you show *me*?" said a voice behind him. The sixth year prefect on dinner duty had come up behind us and neatly plucked the card from the boy's fingers.

The boy stood up quickly.

"Joke," he said, laughing. "Just a joke." He gripped my shoulder tightly. "Wasn't it?"

Total terror filled me. I began to nod my head.

It was Deirdre who spoke up. Little quiet Deirdre who would never open her mouth in primary school.

"No, it wasn't a joke," she said firmly. "He was trying to bully my friend."

("My friend?" I thought. I hadn't known that Deirdre had even liked me at all. However, this was one of those occasions when a person needed every friend they had, so I certainly wasn't arguing.)

Margritte agreed with Deirdre vigorously. "Yes," she said, "he was threatening Mary. And we were told in our secondary school induction training always to tell about bullying 'cos it just gets worse and worse if you don't. And it's very bad for the bully as well, if no one reports them. They will think they can go through life behaving like that. So it has to be stopped. At once."

She gazed righteously at my third year friend.

"It's not good for you," she addressed him firmly, "you'll have bad character formation if no one ever stands up to you."

His mouth had fallen open slightly. He made a soft gurgling noise.

"Is that correct?" asked the sixth year prefect. "Are you forming a bad character?"

The boy smiled a sickly smile at the prefect.

"That card was perfect," he whined. "So she must have grassed. I was a bit annoyed, that's all. I'm on a yellow card from Pa Broon for this."

The prefect examined the card. "She wouldn't have to grass, you plonker. Look at it." He pointed. "Surgery — with a 'j.' No wonder Pa Broon was mad. He's the English principal. Now, get out of my face, or you'll be on a red card from *me*."

"And, hey!" He called after the boy as he was leaving the dinner hall. "Don't go near this lot again. They've got *my* protection."

We gazed at him in adoration.

"He's lovely, isn't he?" said Deirdre.

"He's far too old for you," said Margritte.

(She really could be a little prig at times.)

"What do you think, Mary?" they asked me.

"Mmmm. More mature men can be quite attractive," I said in what I hoped was an enigmatic manner.

I scraped my plate into the massive slop bin full of disgusting half-eaten food and congealed grease, and stacked it with the rest of the dirty dishes and cutlery.

We made for the door. The prefect was chatting to one of the dinner ladies. He glanced at me and beckoned.

"A word," he said.

My heart raced. It *was* a bit early for the Christmas disco but perhaps this would be his introductory move to see if I was prepared to go out with him. What would my mother say? Would I tell her? I sauntered over casually.

He smiled at me in a friendly way as I approached. I tried to smile back as best I could without showing the metal studs. I whipped off my glasses quickly. (I really must pester my mother for a pair of contact lenses, I thought.)

"I worked out how you did it," he indicated the delivery door.

"Oh," I stammered.

He loomed over me. "Skip the dinner queue again," he said, "and I'll chuck you in that slop bin."

26

First year classes were differently divided into various sections for practical subjects. I had science after lunch with a whole new bunch of people. I was really looking forward to this subject. I had a feeling that this would be the one in which I would excel. I have an enquiring mind and am always ready for any experiment. My Uncle Harry has always agreed with me when I say this. My parents usually shudder. So once or twice in the past things sometimes went wrong. We only had to call out the fire brigade once (last year). Who bought me the chemistry set anyway?

I chummed up right away with a few people from different primaries.

"I'm dead keen to get started," I said eagerly, rubbing my hands together. We looked around the lab. There were lots of interesting experiments set up all along the windowsills. "I wonder what we'll get to do first."

"What you will get to do first," said an authoritative voice from the door, "is write out the rules of the lab."

Miss Vincent, our science teacher, gave us each a jotter. By now we were all on automatic pilot. We didn't needed to be told any more. When a jotter was placed in front of us we immediately scribbled furiously on the cover. Our class, year group, subject, classroom number, our own name, teacher's name, and possibly those of any household pets which we might own. We had gone through this rigmarole dozens of times. We knew it off by heart.

"Rules of the lab," dictated Miss Vincent, pacing up and down. "Number one: never, under any circumstances, take out your rulers and underline 'any circumstances,' run in the lab.

"Number two: always follow instructions carefully."

"Number three: when heating anything in a test tube always point the open end of the test tube, begin capital letters, away, end capital letters, from yourself and others.

"Number four: safety goggles must be worn when conducting an experiment."

She paused as someone knocked on the door and came in. It was the lab technician. "May I just have a quick word about the apparatus you wanted set up in lab four?" he asked.

"Certainly."

Miss Vincent cast around for something to keep us occupied while she stepped outside the room for a moment. She picked up a box from her desk. "You may try on your safety goggles while I am away. Mary, you can give them out."

Just because I was giving them out does *not* mean I was responsible for what happened. I mean, it *may* have been my idea to re-enact a scene from *Memphis Belle*. We did all rather resemble World War II air aces with their flying goggles, and when someone started humming the theme from the *Dambusters* it proved too much for me. All my acting instincts rose to the surface and I shouted, "Bandits at twelve o' clock high!"

"Coming out of the sun behind you!" someone else yelled.

Taking evasive action, I threw myself sideways.

I think leaving ongoing experiments set up on windowsills is a pretty stupid thing to do, actually. I didn't point that out to Miss Vincent at the time. She was too busy pointing out to me that I had broken every lab rule which she had just dictated, and had I knocked over sulphuric acid instead of potassium permanganate it wouldn't be bright purple-stained fingers which I would now be waving about, it would be no fingers at all. (I could have made an observation here but I didn't.) And just so that in future I did remember the rules of the lab, I could write them all out ten times tonight and hand them into her tomorrow.

I was also going to mention that I hadn't broken *every* lab rule. I had actually been wearing my safety goggles. But I thought it best not to.

I eventually met up with Jamie in last block that day. French class. Lesson one. We were introduced to the French student.

"The assistant for this year is from the south of France," said the teacher, "near the Spanish border."

A young man, not much older than us, smiled nervously.

"You have to help Jean-Luc with his English as much as he will help you with your French. So please refrain from any local patois, such as 'tatties and mince' for a famous Scottish culinary dish." Monsieur Dijan swept round the class giving out language sheets with spaces to be filled in. "Words like 'knackered' or 'shattered' as a translation for 'exhausted' are specifically forbidden."

He rapped on the table. "Around the wall you will see headsets above ledges. Please take a place and put on the earphones. You are going to hear a tape in French and English, and then you will complete the blank sections on the sheets which you have been given."

Monsieur Dijan wound the tape on the machine at his desk. "I know that you have all done some preparatory language work in primary school so it will not be too difficult."

I got as close as I could to Jamie. "*Merci beaucoup*, a

bunch, for your support in the dinner hall," I said bitterly.

"*Pardon*?" he asked innocently. "*Est-ce que cest un problème?*"

"Don't kid a kidder."

He shuffled his feet.

"Well, there was no point in both of us getting caught. As soon as you started to draw attention to us the Bozo was going to suss right away that we hadn't been at the hatch two seconds earlier. Did he realize how you had got in?"

I was tempted for a second to say no, and let Jamie try the delivery door again and get caught. My unique nobility and sense of loyalty stopped me. "He sure did," I said. "He made a reference to actual physical violence on my person if I did it again."

Jamie was obviously impressed. He whistled.

"Gosh, the warders are threatening the inmates. Wait till I get to be a prefect."

Typical, I thought. Instead of giving me a bit of sympathy and support he thinks of himself. What had impressed me about this character in the first place? I gave him the once over. His appearance had marginally improved, the trousers had been pressed, the jumper was (a little) less scruffy and the earrings had gone. He still didn't look like prefect material to me.

"Ha!" I said scornfully. "I don't see you as a prefect, ever."

"Don't scoff," he said huffily, "maybe I'm a late developer. Our science teacher was telling us about that. Did you know Einstein never passed a maths exam in his life?"

A voice cut across our conversation. "When you are ready, *s'il vous plait*."

27

Jamie and I were leaving the language base at the final
bell when a prefect stopped us. "English principal, Mr
Brown, wants you two. In his room, pronto."

We exchanged glances. Jamie shrugged. "Probably
about the right of way," he said.

"I hope so," I replied.

I was not so sure. It was all right for Jamie to be con-
fident. Matters such as bogus appointment cards,
being caught cheating the dinner queue, friction with
third year pupils, and smashed lab equipment were not
occupying his mind.

There were other reasons than the right of way that
Mr Brown might want to see me about.

I trailed behind Jamie as we made our way to the
English class. Pa Broon had probably changed his
mind regarding the suspect "Surjery Card." Despair
overwhelmed me. He would make an example of me to
serve as a warning for the whole first year.

I tried to remember the discipline procedure which
Mr Wilkins, our form teacher, had so lovingly outlined
on our first day.

For some reason it seemed to be modelled on SFA
rules of conduct for premier league football games.
There were various stages of culpability, involving
punishment exercises, signed and unsigned by parents,
"Doggers' Sheets" and "Behaviour Checks" which
involved being signed in and out of classes by each
teacher, with spaces for comments on conduct. Then
cards of various colours for varying lengths of time,
then suspensions, and then ... out.

I ticked off in my mind all the ones I qualified for so

far. It was quite an impressive score. My parents would
be utterly horrified. All their worst fears were coming
true. I had not "settled down" in secondary school. If
anything I had been involved in more trouble than
before. What I resented most of all was the fact that it
was not my fault at all. Things just happened when I
was there. I must give off negative vibrations or something. There was probably some quite logical explanation which modern science was not advanced enough
yet to reveal. The only person who was likely to believe
that though was my Uncle Harry, and at the moment
he was travelling abroad.

Jamie waited outside the classroom door for me to
catch up with him.

"What's your problem?"

"Oh, I don't know," I mumbled. "Maybe I should go
home sick. I don't fancy a little chat with Pa Broon at
the moment."

"Look," said Jamie, "if this is trouble coming up, I'll
say that I was skipping the dinner queue with you."

"Really?"

I was overwhelmed. As I said at the beginning, I had
had a feeling right from the start that Jamie would be
a good friend. Lately his support had been a bit thin
and I had started to doubt him. One should always go
by your first impressions.

He gave me a rough shove with his rucksack. This I
realized from Jamie was a sign of deep caring. We
opened the door and went in together.

I almost turned round at once and departed. My parents and Jamie's mum and the head teacher were talking to Mr Brown.

"Come in. Come in." The Head waved us through
the doorway.

Jamie and I sidled into the room.

"Mr Brown has just been explaining to me how you two have managed to retrieve valuable historical artefacts. Very commendable."

My father gazed at the ceiling.

It was obvious that Mr Brown had not explained in too great detail exactly how these artefacts had come to be retrieved or we would not be getting such a warm welcome.

"I've had the curator of the Heritage Centre on the phone and she wants to meet both of you. They have removed all the items from the pit and they are now in their basement store. She wants you to come along after school today and have a look at them in a good light and she can take the opportunity to thank you personally."

"I thought I'd contact your parents," Mr Brown said to us, "just in case you were late home from school. You know how parents become concerned when they don't know where their children are." He smiled like the Cheshire cat. "Although I'm sure that you two are much too sensible ever to worry your parents like that."

"Well, I'll leave you to get on with it," said the Head.

He shook everybody by the hand, twice. He managed to pat me on the head. Jamie body-swerved quickly.

"You must be very proud of them," he said.

Jamie's mum nodded.

My parents gave him a fixed smile.

Mr Brown sniggered. He pretended it was a sneeze. But I heard him.

28

The curator of the Heritage Centre came to meet us as we entered the foyer. By the way she acted you would think someone had just deposited the Honours of Scotland on her.

"The best find we've had in ages," she said enthusiastically. "It may actually have been beneficial for the material to have been buried so long in that pit. The inscriptions are very well preserved."

She beamed at my parents.

"You must be very proud of your children."

My mother gazed at her in alarm. I don't know whether it was because she thought the curator might possibly be including Jamie as one of her "children." Or whether the fact that when they nearly got themselves buried alive by indulging in dangerous activities one should be proud of one's offspring's exploits. Anyway, she regarded Ms Morgan in the manner as one might regard someone who was slightly soft in the head.

The curator led us downstairs to where the mortsafe and the other articles were laid out. They had been numbered and tagged, and I must admit appeared more friendly and interesting in the bright lights of the museum store. I touched one of the pieces of headstone. It was very cold.

"It is not just having the actual piece of stone as another part of our collection" said Ms Morgan. "These finds are important as they shed light on our history."

She told us that it was usually local masons who would carve a headstone and although there were sometimes not of the best artistic quality they still managed to make each grave special. Tablestones were still in use in the eighteenth century but they were becoming less common. The masons therefore had to rethink their designs, because what was suitable for a slab would not always do for a headstone. To represent Death they used symbols such as a scythe, a skull and bones, a coffin, and ones for Time such as an hourglass. Winged souls, as an emblem of immortality, were very common. Many tombstones had sculptures of the trade of the deceased on them. This was a very old practice; there are examples of this in the catacombs in Rome. It was of great interest to her as it would give historians more local information. She had an example of a watch-maker's headstone with its hammer, pliers and tweezers.

"Studies of this type of material are absolutely absorbing," she said.

Jamie was nodding his head. This was his kind of conversation.

Ms Morgan explained about restoration techniques and how to conserve certain types of articles properly they had to be kept under specific conditions. I hadn't realized that there was a whole science to it. Humidity and exposure to sunlight had to be carefully moni-tored. She brought out some old books and explained how "foxing" occurred due to the chemical reactions in the paper.

"Some items are unique," she said, "for example the town's royal charter. In the case of certain historical artefacts we don't get a second chance. There are no replacements available. It is quite a responsibility."

She showed them the back files of newspapers, the old burgh record books and the census material.

Jamie was fascinated. I thought it was mildly inter-esting, but he was completely taken with it all. "I think I could make a career here," he said eventually.

We all paused, waiting for the curator to scream or faint or make some feeble protest at least.

She patted him on the back enthusiastically. "Great news," she said. "I love to hear someone say that. Most people think work like this is boring. They just don't appreciate the hundreds of absorbing little details involved."

She turned to Mr Brown. "It's good to know that there are some young people who will carry on with the type of work which we know to be so important. Isn't it?"

Mr Brown gave a non-committal grunt.

There was no stopping her. "The school pupils have to do some work experience, don't they? I believe that it is compulsory for each child to experience actual employment in local industry or with firms and offices. This would be an ideal placement for Jamie when his turn came up."

Mr Brown gave a small yelp. "That's thinking a bit far ahead for this age group. Some of them haven't quite mastered the art of getting themselves to the correct school at the correct time yet." He deliberately avoided looking at me. "We don't release them upon the general public until a little later."

"Well, you know that there is a vacancy here for Jamie when the time comes."

My mother's first impression had been correct. The curator was no judge of character at all. She would have been far better asking for someone more reliable from the school. Someone such as myself.

29

"He doesn't look like a farmer to me," Jamie whispered, "not a proper one, anyway."

We were in the district council headquarters a few weeks later and the person Jamie was referring to was sitting opposite us. He had on a trendy suit and shades. I actually thought he looked quite sharp, especially with the shades.

"How did you expect him to dress for this? Like Wurzel Gummidge?"

I had thought the farmer had acted fairly reasonably in letting Mr Brown and some of the museum staff get the archaeological stuff (and Jamie) out of his pit before he had filled it in.

"Quieten down, you two," said Mr Brown. "Pay close attention to what goes on. You are not getting time off school for nothing. This is a valuable experience for you. I will ask you both questions later. It will give you an insight into how local government works, or doesn't," he added under his breath. He gave Jamie's mother, who was sitting beside him, an encouraging smile.

Jamie made a gesture behind his back as though he was going to throw up.

"I think I shall start by introducing everyone," said the man from the planning department. "And then we can get down to business."

The preamble went on and on, about rights of the public and tolerance of landowners, and uninterrupted periods of use and recent changes in the law regarding the aforesaid.

Jamie and I studiously avoided looking at each other

when they mentioned users not causing distress to animals, and leaving gates open. Though strictly speaking we hadn't actually left the gate open, as we had climbed over it in the first place. The farmer kept saying it was his land and he should be able to decide what to do with it, and he couldn't allow people to wander about at any time of the day or night. And also his bull had been unwell after that experience.

At this point Jamie suggested innocently that perhaps maybe he should move his bull to another field as perhaps something it was eating in that particular field had disagreed with it.

The farmer gave Jamie and me a very nasty look, and added that farms were dangerous places, and any ignorant people who went messing around on his property in future did so at their own risk.

Mr Brown then got ratty and said by blocking up the bit in the graveyard wall, where the old stile had been, the farmer had caused a wilful obstruction, and the community council were going to petition the district council to initiate legal proceedings to have the route reopened.

One up for us!

The farmer asked the planning officer if they could do that and he said yes but the point of this meeting was to see if some compromise could be reached. "Persuasion through dialogue," it is known as. This was one of my parents' methods of getting me to do something I didn't want to. I began to feel sorry for the farmer. Up against Mr Brown he didn't have a chance.

Mr Brown had had a survey done by environmentalists. The lane area was positively crammed with wild flowers — poppies, blue cornflower and corn marigolds. He showed everyone some lovely colour photographs of the undergrowth in our lane. Also, and here he glanced triumphantly at Jamie's mother — we had proof positive that this particular path belonged to our ancient national and local heritage.

The museum staff believed that the large stone retrieved from the farmer's pit was the original "Coffin Stone" and had been dumped there to help fill up the hole and clear the gully. The gully was the dried-up bed of the old river and, long ago, burial parties would cross there at the ford on their way to the cemetery. Jamie's grandfather and great-grandfather had kept diaries and accounts which detailed this. Jamie's mother brought out the map, and documents and letters she had found among their family papers. Mr Brown had carefully catalogued them all and presented the planning officer with an annotated list.

The planning officer was very impressed. The farmer looked stunned but he was still determined. "All this makes no difference," he said stubbornly, "the land is mine for whatever use I want to put it to."

It was at this moment that Jamie did his Baldric imitation.

"I have a plan," he said.

I distinctly heard Mr Brown groan. I was sitting right next to him so I should know. He covered it up quickly with a cough when Jamie's mum said, "Oh, good. Let's hear Jamie's idea."

This in itself is evidence that mothers are in some way besotted with male offspring. If I had come out with a statement like that both my parents would have immediately said, "Be quiet, Mary."

In the manner of one of Wellington's generals unfurling his battle map for Waterloo, Jamie brought his sketches out of his rucksack.

"What we can do is look at this from a different viewpoint. What you might call lateral thinking," he said importantly. "There is always another way to do something, apart from the most obvious. After all, one doesn't need to rush bullheaded at things."

He was taking a risk with that little remark I thought. I saw my father's eyes widen and the farmer's face went pink.

"What I propose is that we alter the line of the path where the lane meets the field." He indicated the point on his map. "It would curve round instead of going diagonally across the field. Then following the line of the graveyard wall exit approximately here." He spread more maps across the table. "I have traced the appropriate lines here."

He produced "before" and "after" maps and then sat back looking enormously pleased with himself. He was beginning to irritate me the teensiest little bit.

"Now let me see if I have got all this," said the planning offer, who had been scribbling furiously all this time. "You are suggesting a path on the perimeter of the land and then establishing a right of way through the lane and *round* the field, meeting up at the graveyard wall?"

He hesitated for a moment. "Mmmm. You know, it just might work."

What a cliché. Who was writing the lines for him?

The farmer muttered and grumbled but indicated he might accept it.

"There is a story about one of the American presidents," said Jamie's mother suddenly. "He was asked to open a new university campus and the dean complained to him about how the students were ruining the beautiful lawns and gardens by walking across them instead of using the proper laid-out paths. And do you know what the Amerian President said?" She paused. "He said, 'Why don't you make the paths where the students want to walk?.'"

There was a silence for about a minute. Mr Brown gazed at her in admiration.

The planning officer cleared his throat. "That is all very well," he said, "but we have to come to some agreement here that is suitable to both parties. I will have to check all this out with other departments but I think Jamie has a point. It would be best to realign the path. This would make a right of way and give the farmer his field back."

"It is just looking at a problem from every angle," said Jamie in stupid fake and pretentiously modest manner.

"Well done, Jamie," his mum said proudly.

"The most direct approach is not always the best one," the little twerp went on. "there is usually more than one way to do something. All it takes is some independent thinking."

"Hang on a minute," I said. There was something beginning to strike me as being slightly familiar about all of this. 'this is actually my idea. Isn't it?" I asked him.

"What?" said Jamie, a little startled.

"*My* idea," I repeated. "If not the technical details, then certainly this thinking behind the approach to the problem."

Jamie put on one of his blank stares.

"Remember in the dinner hall queue?" I said. "*You* were for barging straight in, and I said sometimes the most direct route was not the best way."

"Oh, yes?" said Mr Brown leaning forward in interest.

I wittered on unaware. "I said that a different approach was needed. I explained about independent thinking. It was *me* who said, 'let's go round by the yard and come in from the side' ... I trailed off.

Jamie smirked.

"Oh, so that's what you two are up to," said Mr Brown.

"Well, I suppose it does show enterprise," said my father.

The planning officer sensed a row developing. He spoke quickly, "Well, it certainly seems to offer a solution here," he said. "Leave it with me and I'll be in touch with all of you shortly."

As we filed out I managed to kick Jamie quite hard.

"Hurry up, Mary, or we will be late," my mother shouted up the stairs.

I was standing in front of my bedroom mirror trying to decide between my red-framed reactolite rapides, or a pair of Duane Wayne flip-up shades. I chose the flip-ups.

"Coming," I called.

Mr parents were waiting in the hall for me. My father was barely passable with his good suit. But my mother! She was wearing a flowery dress and a *hat*!

"We are only going to the opening of the path," I said.

"It's the official opening of the new walkway and the provost will be there," said my mother. "Some of us like to be respectably dressed." She frowned and looked at me.

I was wearing a bright red sweatshirt and jeans. "I'm not changing," I said mulishly.

"Nobody asked you to," said my father pleasantly. He was in one of his "let's humour her" moods. "Come on, get in the car."

Only *my* parents would think of *driving* to the opening of a new walkway.

Mr Brown waved us over as soon as we arrived. They had hung balloons and bunting all around the place. People were milling about in confusion but you could recognize the provost. He had on his gold chain.

"How much do you think that is worth?" Jamie asked me.

I didn't answer him. Perhaps I should have paid more attention. Both of us were to find out much later

that it was valuable enough for someone to steal it, but
I'll have to tell you about that in another book. At the
time I was too busy taking in the "new walkway."

We had all been actively involved in constructing the
new path. It was actually quite interesting to find out
all the sorts of things that are involved in what seemed
a straightforward project, surveying the land, drainage
and moving topsoil. Things like choosing suitably
strong yet visually attractive fencing is an art in itself.
They called in the experts to advise them on moving
delicate plants and making a minimum of disturbance
to any wildlife using the area. Jamie's grandad turned
out to be very knowledgeable about wildflowers and
skilled in design. He spent hours sketching out different ideas. Jamie's mum said it was the best thing that
had happened to him in years. Jamie said it was worth
it for him to get time off school at any rate.

Then we all received letters inviting us to the official
opening.

They had broken through the gap in the hedges and
made a proper entrance to the lane. The gully had been
filled in and the undergrowth cut back and a paved path
laid out. It led all the way down and then turned sharp
right along the edge of the field, then left for a little way
to a different opening in the graveyard wall. They had
very carefully moved the old stile stone by stone and
rebuilt it down a fair bit. It would lead into a different
part among the tombs. I suppose it would give Kathleen
Campbell a bit of peace, but I had a feeling she liked the
company. I would have to go back and visit her.

"That farmer's made a good deal," said Jamie. "He
has got a new fence and an extra bit of ground. And I
have to walk further and the winter is coming."

I was going to point out that it was only a few yards
further and it had been *his* idea, but I decided not to.

We walked on. We looked at the artistically designed archway leading in from the road. That had been Jamie's idea, no more scrambling through hedges disturbing the wildlife.

"Once that weathers a bit it will look okay," said Jamie, studying it critically.

I had to agree. Next we had the different tones of paving stones on the lane leading down to the field. That had been my contribution. The planning staff and I had some really lively discussions before settling on the most suitable tones to complement the surrounding terrain. I must confess I was a little put out when they wouldn't agree to have a couple of bright purple hexagons just to liven up the look of the place.

Actually, environmental planning is quite an interesting subject. I told the council's planning officer that I was thinking of making it my career. He said not to be too hasty and that I was far too young to make decisions like that just yet.

I must admit that their design seemed to blend in rather well with the banks of wildflowers, the yarrow and the ox-eye daisies.

"Not bad," said Jamie grudgingly.

"Yes," I said, "and it's all due to us."

We wandered back. My parents were chatting to Mr Brown and Jamie's mum. Goodness knows what my mother thought of her gear for the occasion. She was wearing jeans and a sweatshirt. Grandad James was there in his wheelchair. He looked really smart in a white high collar shirt with studs and a black suit and tie. He was waving his stick about and explaining to my father about soil conditions and rare wild plants. Mr Brown had started calling Jamie's mother by her first name. Jamie glowered.

"There you are," Mr Brown said very chummily.

"They are about to start. Oh, by the way, there is some-one here you might know. She joined the community council when she retired, another teacher I'm afraid." He motioned to someone in the crowd, who waved and came over.

The bodies parted and I was face to face with Mrs Cult, my ex-drama teacher.

My mother said later it was surprising that the woman didn't faint clean away because she was ninety-nine per cent sure it was because of me that Mrs Cult had taken early retirement. I suppose she was refer-ring to the Christmas pageant — the one Mrs Cult had put on for my primary school's jubilee. There were a lot of important people in the audience that night, the Director of Education, local clergy, and so on. I don't know what all the commotion was about. My Uncle Harry said it was by far the best Christmas play he had ever seen in the whole of his life.

I flipped my Duane Wayne shades at her and said, "Hello."

"Why, Mary," she said in surprise. I noticed that her voice trembled slightly and her hands started to shake a little. She was probably getting quite emo-tional at seeing one of her former pupils. I'm sure that when teachers retire they really miss their favourite ones.

"How are you getting on at secondary school?" she said.

"Terrific!" I answered enthusiastically. "No problem. I ..."

I just happened to catch Mr Brown's eye at this point.

"Mary and Jamie are settling in very well," he said. "They are both quite ... 'interesting' ... pupils to have in one's class."

"You mean there's another one like her?" I heard Mrs Cult whisper as they moved away.

I hadn't really been fibbing when I had said it was terrific. Apart from one or two little hiccups to begin with I was enjoying secondary school. The varied subjects with different teachers, moving class each block, making new friends and getting to know the people from primary school much better. It was great.

The provost coughed loudly and declared the walkway open and pulled a little curtain back from a plaque set in a stone.

"Coffin Walk" it said. They had wanted to call it something flowery like Daisy Path, but Jamie insisted. It was for his grandad he said.

The provost decided to make a speech although no one was listening. He went on about our heritage and how people shouldn't forget that it was this district council who had built the Heritage Centre and done this work. Despite the cutbacks of the present government they would be doing even more exciting things, and my father muttered, "Oh, so that is where our tax money is going."

Mr Brown was studying the line of the path, checking they had got it right. He seemed satisfied. "This shows that imaginative planning can improve the environment and not destroy it," he declared.

Jamie nudged me. We sidled down the path. I suppose we should have noticed that the gate to the field had been left slightly ajar. We went past it and climbed over the stile. I glanced over at Kathleen's grave.

"Listen," Jamie said, "do you know the place at the old railway line where the burn flows under the canal? Well, I was down there yesterday and I found this tunnel. I think it's a shortcut to somewhere. I'll show you if you like."

We sat on the wall for a minute. Away to our left the flags fluttered in the wind. The dignitaries all had their backs to us, chatting and laughing. The bull was grazing at the far end of the field. Perhaps we were upwind or maybe it was that sixth sense which animals are supposed to have. Anyway, it looked up and focused on us, then it started stamping and pawing the ground a bit. I wondered later if it had remembered the pain of being zapped, or whether it just behaved according to its own natural instincts. (We did a module in biology later about genetic programming that made me consider this as an explanation for what happened.)

I had a soft spot for that old bull. I stood up on the wall and gave it a big farewell wave. *Honestly*, I completely forgot that I was wearing a bright red sweatshirt!

"Come on," said Jamie and pulled my arm.

We jumped down and ran off through the graveyard.

Behind us in the field the bull spied the flapping bunting and the open gate. It lowered its head and charged.

Simon's Challenge

Theresa Breslin

All that Simon really wants is a computer. However, with his father away looking for work and a new baby in the house, money is tight.

One evening, Simon passes Mr Peterson's computer shop. Everything seems normal. But when the police start asking questions, Simon realizes that he may have witnessed a major burglary. The only problem is that he can't remember any details ...

For more information, book notes and activities check out **www.theresabreslin.com**

Kelpies

Different Directions

Theresa Breslin

No one should have to help their own mother with her maths homework!

Okay, so Katharine's mother wants to go back to school but did she have to choose *her* school? Her friends all think Mrs Douglas is great, but Katharine feels embarrassed, especially when she hears rumours about her mother and Hedgehog, the maths teacher. As if she hasn't got enough problems of her own!

But then Katharine learns something about her mother which puts everything else into perspective, and unexpectedly brings them closer together.

For more information, book notes and activities check out **www.theresabreslin.com**

Kelpies